A SALACIOUS SCANDAL AND STEAK SIZZLERS

to move fast over the years. Not her fault really. She just gets distracted by an interesting scent and completely forgets that her toy exists and then goes to pee on the interesting scent without thinking about the fact that she dropped the toy where the scent was in order to better smell it.

And, of course, I enable her by swooping in to grab her toy before she actually pees on it so she never "learns her lesson", which, I mean really, she's a dog. That sort of thing doesn't work well with them anyway.

So.

I had just swooped in and grabbed her toy before she could pee on it when I realized we weren't alone.

There was a very shaggy, large, scary man standing about four feet away from us.

"Hello," he said in a deep voice.

"Hello," I replied with false cheer as I casually looked around to see if there was anyone around, anywhere at all. (There was not.)

I tried not to flinch as he took a step closer, holding out a hand for Fancy to sniff, and I recognized him.

Creek is a small town. Even if you don't know someone, you know them. And the man who I was suddenly very alone with, Evan Browers, was someone my grandma and grandpa had told me to avoid from the time I could first leave the house on my own.

Even before that, really. Because I'd never seen my grandpa talk to the man and you have to understand that my grandpa is an ex-con, so he's not exactly the look-down-on-others type. He's seen rough times and is far more likely to put a hand out to lift someone up than to push them down. So the fact that he avoided this man meant something.

I hadn't actually grown up in Creek so I didn't know precisely what he'd done, I just knew he was the embodiment of Stranger Danger and I was suddenly all alone with him.

Fancy, being Fancy, had proceeded from sniffing his hand to licking his beard, which meant there went my "I have a big scary dog you better back off" plan.

He stood back up and stared at me a little longer than was polite. "You're Maggie May Carver."

"I am."

My instincts were saying "run away screaming" but my polite upbringing was saying "that would be an awfully rude thing to do" especially when I didn't even know what he'd done. Maybe he wasn't a killer. Or a rapist. Maybe he was just some weird man with bad social skills who rubbed people the wrong way.

And maybe there was nothing to the fact that he'd randomly chanced upon me when I was all alone. He could be perfectly harmless.

Yeah, right. That was it.

(I was so dead.)

He took another step closer and I could smell a slight whiff of mustiness like he'd put on clothes that had never quite dried out. Eau de backpacker. "I need your help," he said.

It took everything I had not to step back. "Mine? What for? What can *I* do to help you?"

I mean, I was a former barkery owner and future pet resort owner. Not exactly "help someone" professions. And I was pretty sure he didn't need my consulting skills. He didn't look like the type who needed a hundred-page written report with fifty bullet-pointed items for improvement ranked from essential to nice-to-have.

He crossed his arms and rocked back on his heels. "I want you to investigate the murder of Mary Diever."

Oh, that made more sense. I had sort of solved a handful of murders and found a kid's missing mom. And it had been written up in the local paper so it made sense that he'd know about it. Which meant maybe I was going to survive until dinner. How nice.

"Mary Diever? Who is that?" I tried to think if I'd heard of any murders recently, but drew a blank.

"Mary Diever is the woman everyone thinks I killed thirty-six years ago."

"Oh."

Well, that explained why everyone stayed away from him.

"So you didn't kill her?" I asked.

He stared at me for a long moment, but this time it wasn't the stare of a man with bad social skills. No, it was the stare of a man wondering just how stupid I was. "No. I didn't kill her."

"But then…I mean, thirty-six years. Why now?" (And why stop me in the freezing cold of November to ask about it. I mean, seriously. My toes were turning into little rocks.) "And why me? Why not just ask the cops to take another look?"

He shoved his hands into his pockets. "You know what, forget it. I thought you'd be different, not having grown up here. But, just…" He shook his head and started to turn away.

I knew I was going to regret it, but I'm a sucker for people in need. Even big scary men who could snap me in two with half a thought and who I've been warned are dangerous. (I tell ya, I would've so fallen for Ted Bundy's "help me with these groceries" bit.)

"Wait," I said. "Do you want to come back to the house and tell me what's going on? I have coffee. Or tea."

Yes, it probably wasn't the best idea to invite this strange man that no one trusted back to my house when no one would know that we'd even crossed paths and he could easily murder me and be about his day without anyone noticing.

But I go with my gut. And the more I was around the guy I suspected that he was just one of those people who don't interact with others much and so was really awkward when he did. I didn't get that Ted Little vibe off of him.

Plus, Fancy had laid herself down by his side. She clearly wasn't the least bit concerned about him. And dogs are pretty good judges of character in my experience. At least, if a dog doesn't like someone, you should run. They can sometimes like very flawed people, but I've never seen a situation where a dog didn't like a particular person and was wrong about it.

So, yes, it was a risk to invite him into my home. But I lived next to my grandpa, and a few blocks from the police station where Matt was working, and at least I'd be warm if I was going to be brutally murdered.

Plus I was craving some of that peanut butter fudge I'd made the night before. I'd added a dash of red pepper flakes and they'd really kicked the flavor up a notch.

"Come on." I took a step towards my house, but Fancy stayed where she was lying at his feet. (Such a traitor. I swear she loves any man more than me.)

He pressed his lips together and stared at me intently before nodding. "Okay."

Maybe the local pastor takes some pity on you, because that's what they do. Or the local thugs. (Because there are always local thugs of one sort or another.) But probably not a lot of good, upstanding citizens reaching out to make you welcome.

So if it turns out you really are a nice guy who's just a bit awkward, what does that life look like? Pretty sad and lonely if I had to guess.

As I brought out the container of fudge from the fridge and turned to prepare myself a cup of hot chocolate, I hoped he wasn't going to turn out to be a murderer after all. It would suck to learn that about him now that I'd put myself in his shoes.

"So? Drink?" I asked, trying to restart the awkward conversation.

"I wouldn't mind a hot chocolate."

"Great. And, please, help yourself to some of that fudge or else I'm likely to eat the whole thing myself."

He glanced at the container which probably had a good forty pieces in it. "You'd eat all of that yourself?"

I tilted my head to the side. "Well, maybe not all of it, today, but probably half of it, yeah. I mean, it's rich, so I really can't eat more than one or two pieces at a time. But it's also really good so I keep going back for more. I'd say working from home is bad for my health, but honestly I was even worse at the barkery. Jamie can cook a mean dessert."

"Oh yeah, I heard about that place. Did you really open a bakery for dogs?"

I smiled. "I did. And we were doing well, too. Until someone decided to tear the building we were renting down. But we'll be reopening next summer as part of a whole pet resort. Assuming the world hasn't burned to the ground by then, of course." I grabbed a piece of fudge and savored its creamy flavor as I contemplated the current messed up state of the world.

He took a piece, too. "Doubt it'll get that bad. People always pull through."

The microwave beeped and I poured hot water over the chocolate powder in our cups and stirred each one before handing him his. "You sound like my grandpa. Always looking on the bright side."

"Not surprising. He's seen some things, too. You either look on the bright side or it takes you down."

(He didn't actually use the word *things*, but I'm trying to keep it polite here. Not that I was bothered by that little s-word. I've used far worse in my time. And he was right, my grandpa really had seen some *things* in his life.)

I settled down at the table and took a long sip of my hot chocolate, savoring how the heat spread through my chest and the cup warmed my hands. "So. Tell me why now? Why me? Why not ask the cops to take another look? Why not just let it go after all these years?"

He stared at his cup, his large hands dwarfing the sturdy ceramic as he cradled it between them. "The cops did reopen the case. They took my DNA yesterday. They're going to send it off to a lab."

I set down the piece of fudge I'd been about to shove in my mouth. "And…"

He sighed and finally looked up at me. "And it's going to match. That's why I need your help."

I smiled nervously. Oh, goodie. I was drinking hot chocolate with a killer.

CHAPTER 4

"I'm confused," I finally managed. "If it's going to match, then didn't you…"

He leaned forward, resting his elbows on the table. "I didn't kill her. But the stupid cops are going to think I did. I was just, with her."

"Right. How foolish of them. To think that the man whose DNA was on her when she was found was the man who killed her."

I didn't mean it to come out sounding all condescending, but I mean, come on.

What were they supposed to think? Words are nice and all, but put some good old-fashioned DNA evidence up there on the board and pretty much everyone is going to believe in that result a lot more than someone's word that they didn't do it.

Especially someone without any built-up goodwill who everyone already thought did it.

He glared at me, but not with that quick-spike sort of anger that some men have that makes me want to flinch because I know they're capable of harm.

No, this was more along the lines of my grandpa who

Aleksa Baxter

can glare me down with the best of them when I say
something particularly ignorant or foolish. So I sat back
and took a deep breath.

"Okay. Let's start over here, Mr. Browers," I said.
"You obviously knew Mary Diever."

"Yes. And, please, call me Evan."

"Okay, Evan. *How* exactly did you know Mary
Diever? You said you were with her, what does that
mean exactly?"

Before he could answer, someone knocked on my
front door and then opened it. Had to be my grandpa.
He was the only one who'd just let himself in like that.
Fancy ran to greet him.

"Hey Grandpa, we're in the kitchen," I called

He came through the door from the living room,
dressed in work boots, jeans, and a long-sleeved red and
black-checkered flannel shirt. He hadn't even bothered
to put on a hat or gloves. I should get *him* to walk Fancy.
Not that he'd see the point in taking a dog for a walk for
fun. Dogs were meant to have a purpose in his world, not
be some sort of surrogate child.

At first glance, my grandpa appeared to be about the
same age as Evan Browers even though he was over
eighty and Evan had to be in his sixties. Part of it was
down to the fact that his hair was still a light brown
instead of gray and he'd always stayed trim. But the
years were there, hiding in the wrinkles around his eyes
and the way he limped a bit on really cold mornings.

He turned all of his attention on Evan Browers, but
before he could say something cutting, I jumped in.
"Grandpa, have you met Evan Browers? Mr. Browers,
this is my grandpa, Lou Carver."

Evan nodded to my grandpa. "Mr. Carver. Sir."

"What are you doing here?" my grandpa demanded, not moving from the doorway, his arms crossed across his chest, legs planted shoulder width apart.

That wasn't good. My grandpa had done fifteen years in prison for armed robbery. I'd never seen him be violent, but I knew he was capable of it. You don't survive that long in that kind of environment without learning how to defend yourself, and his stance said he was ready for a fight.

"Grandpa. Back off. Mr. Browers here has asked for my help. He wants me to find who killed Mary Diever."

"I'll give you a clue. You're sitting across from him right now."

I saw that look cross Evan's face, the one that had flashed across it right before he turned to walk away from me outside. "Grandpa! Sit. Give the man a chance to tell his story. Unless you were there? Did you actually see him kill her?"

My grandpa hesitated in the doorway for another moment but he finally joined us at the table, dragging his chair around next to me until he was facing Evan Browers. "Fine. Tell your story. Convince me you didn't murder that young lady."

"Grandpa," I warned.

He raised an eyebrow in my direction, but he didn't drop the menacing glare.

"Mr. Browers, I'm sorry. Please. Tell us what happened back then. And tell us why they're going to find your DNA on her even though that doesn't mean you killed her. I mean, don't they usually send off something intimate in these situations? Not just something a passerby could've touched? And if you were, um, intimate with her, why didn't you tell anyone back then?"

My grandpa snorted in disbelief at my gullibility, but he didn't say anything more, just continued to glare at Evan as the big man turned his coffee cup in his hands and searched for the right words to convince us to help him.

CHAPTER 5

Evan finally looked up and met my grandpa's glare, eye for eye. "I didn't kill Mary."

My grandpa pursed his lips, but didn't say anything.

"Look, I'm not a saint, never have been. Hell, I don't even like most people. But I'd never hurt a woman. And Mary…Mary was an angel. She was my angel."

"Wait one sec." I ran to my room and grabbed a spiral-bound notebook and a pen. "Okay, sorry. Go. You knew Mary…"

He smiled softly. "Yeah, I knew Mary. I was in love with her. Everyone was. But, more importantly, she was in love with me."

My grandpa snorted at that.

"I know. Hard to believe. Me, a no-good loser who'd been in trouble with the law and only got by scraping together the odd job here or there. And Mary, who'd been to college, and whose father was a lawyer, and who lived in a house with more rooms than most hotels. But it's true."

My grandpa shook his head. "She was at least a decade younger than you."

"More. Twelve years."

"But you're telling me she loved you. You got any proof of that?" he asked, not letting up for a moment.

Evan focused on the coffee cup once more. "I have a photo of us. A Polaroid where she was asleep on my chest."

"Mmhm. And why didn't you give it to the cops? Tell them you were involved? Let them know they were looking at the wrong man?"

Evan shoved back from the table and crossed his arms. "Because then they would've arrested me for sure. You know how small a place this was thirty-six years ago. Everybody assumed they knew exactly what was going on with everyone else. They would've never believed me. And her daddy…No way he would've believed it. And him a big lawyer like that? I would've spent the rest of my life in prison."

I leaned forward. "So you lied to the cops when they asked you about her?"

He nodded. "I had to."

"And the DNA?" I asked.

"Well, we'd been together, hadn't we? That morning. She met me down by the river in this little spot we had. And then I left and went about my day, didn't think anything of it. We had plans to meet back there in three more days, but that afternoon someone said she was missing. Didn't take long to find her body."

"How close was it to the spot where you guys would meet?"

He huffed out a breath. "About a hundred feet away. Which is probably why the cops jumped to all the wrong conclusions. They found our spot. And they assumed that what happened there was part of her murder."

I glanced at my grandpa and then at Mr. Browers. I really didn't know how to delicately ask what I needed to ask. And I really didn't want to ask it at all in front of my grandpa. But, I needed to know.

"Um, so, when you two were…together…" I realized I'd intermeshed my fingers as I said the words, blushed deep scarlet, and dropped my hands into my lap. "Um…Were you, by any chance, um, rough with her? I mean, in a way that the cops would mistake for, you know, rape?"

I had to force myself to look at him instead of away. Some topics are so darned awkward. But I needed to see his face and his reaction if I was going to believe what he told me.

He recoiled slightly. "No. I mean…no. We…no."

"So no grabbing her arms too tight or," I cleared my throat, "um, choking, or anything?"

"Maggie May," my grandpa snapped at me.

"What? Some people…enjoy certain things. And maybe in an autopsy they look bad. So if that's the case then we need to know that."

Evan shook his head. "No. Nothing like that. I swear. Just…sex."

"Okay. Good. That helps. I mean, if there were any signs like that then we know the killer left them. And if there weren't then that supports your story. That's good. Either way."

I ran a hand through my hair, wondering why it felt like there was so much of it these days. Getting old is weird. But I put that aside, I had a murder to focus on. "So, if it wasn't you, who do you think it was?"

He turned the coffee cup around and around for a good minute.

"Mr. Browers?"

"Evan, please." He frowned at the table for a moment before saying, "Mary was a good girl."

I tried to catch his eye. "A good girl who was sneaking away to have sex with her much older and rougher around the edges boyfriend. Evan, what else was she into that no one knew about?"

He ran his hands through his hair and dropped them to the table. "It wasn't like that. I mean, it was just a little, a little hash. And maybe she tried cocaine once or twice."

Oh, is that all? I thought to myself. *Just a little cocaine. No biggie.* It always amazes me what vastly different perspectives people have. To me there is no such thing as "a little" cocaine. Or a little hash for that matter. I am such a prude.

"Where did she do this? Who with? You?"

He looked like he wanted to run away again.

"Mr. Browers. Evan. If you want me to find her real killer you have to tell me the truth about her so I can figure out who else might've done it. Did she do these things with you? Or did she do them with others?"

He licked his lips. "With others. I'd...I'd had my party days. I got clean in jail and stayed clean."

"Do you know who these others were?"

He shook his head.

"So how did you know about it?"

"She showed up high a few times. And when I asked her about it, she said it wasn't a big deal. Not something she did often."

"Okay." I jotted that down. "Tell me, how did you meet?"

22

"I picked up some general repair work around her daddy's house." He shrugged a shoulder. "We met when she came back to live there for the summer. Got to talking one day when he wasn't around. Hit it off. And then, she kissed me."

My grandpa snorted.

"Grandpa."

"What? You never saw Mary Diever. Pale blonde curly hair around these big blue eyes. Soft-spoken. So quiet you had to lean in to hear what she was saying. Couldn't have been an inch over five foot. And this lout wants us to believe *she* kissed *him*."

"She did."

"Prove it." My grandpa jutted his chin out in challenge as I snagged another piece of fudge and studied Evan Browers.

"I can't. That's why I never told anyone." He glanced towards the door.

"Running won't help, you know," I told him. "It'll just make you look even guiltier."

He smiled at me and I saw a little hint of what Mary Diever might've seen all those years ago. "What are you, a mind reader?" he asked.

"No. Just very good at putting myself in someone else's shoes and trying to think what I'd do in their place. So. She kissed you. And then?"

"And then something started between us. It was…intense."

I jotted that down, too. "How long were you together before she was killed?"

"About six weeks."

"She told you about some of the other things she was

up to, like the drugs. Do you think she told anyone else about you?"

He shook his head. "I don't think so. We agreed to keep it between us. At least until…"

"Until?"

"She was talking about marriage. I mean, can't keep that secret, can you?"

"No, not if you want to actually live together. So no friends she'd confide in?"

"No. None. Look. I want to be clear on something. Mary was a good girl."

It was my turn to snort. "Mr. Browers, I'm not going to judge her for what she did. That's her choice, her business. I've known really decent people who did far worse than that. But, let's be real here. From what you've told me, Mary was sneaking around doing drugs and hanging out with questionable people. Not just you, but whoever was supplying those drugs. That's not a 'good girl' in my books. I've known plenty of women with soft voices and big eyes who were manipulative snakes in the grass."

I held up a hand before he could interrupt and defend her. "I'm not saying she was like that. But from what you've told us it sounds like she was in the midst of a little rebellion and you were one part of how she was acting out. Is there anything else we need to know?"

"No." But he frowned and looked away.

"Mr. Browers? Evan? What is it that you're not telling us?"

He pressed his lips together. "I heard her and her father talking one day. Made me think that maybe there was someone else or had been. She wouldn't speak about it when I asked her, but I know what I heard."

"A jealous ex is a good suspect. Do you think that's why she was keeping her relationship with you a secret?"

"No. That was her father. He'd never approve. He wanted more for his daughter than someone like me."

"But you said she was talking marriage."

"She mentioned it sometimes. Running away together. I didn't really believe her, though." He studied the table, not making eye contact. "I always told her if she found someone better than me she should go for it."

I raised my eyebrows. "I thought you loved her."

He glared at me. "I did. Which is why I knew I wasn't the right man for her. She had so much potential. I was willing to take any moment she'd give me, but I knew eventually she'd wake up and walk away. I didn't want to be the one who tied her to a small life when she could have the world."

I barely managed not to roll my eyes. (It's a personal thing. I'd had a guy or two pull that, "if you find someone else" line on me. But what they didn't realize is that while they were there being all noble I was just left alone because there wasn't anyone else I wanted to be with at the time and they certainly weren't going all in themselves, now were they? Men and their mixed up notions…I was so glad I'd found Matt and would never have to deal with any of that mess again. If he left me I was just going to join a convent, lack of religious calling notwithstanding.)

"Did she have a diary?" I asked.

"Not that I know of."

I drummed my pen against the notepad, trying to think of any other questions to ask, but nothing came to mind.

I took a deep breath and sighed as I stared at what little we did have. "Okay. Let me see if I can sum this up. All the physical evidence will point to you. Most people already think you did it. As far as you know, there's no one else who knows that you two were involved. And even if they did it was a situation where someone could accuse you of killing her when she tried to leave you. Or when you found out that she'd been involved with some other man she wouldn't tell you about."

I took another piece of fudge (only my fifth or sixth) and popped it in my mouth as I contemplated the likelihood that Evan Browers was going to spend the rest of his life in prison even if he was innocent.

I didn't see how he was going to get out of this. Then again, at least there was nothing to lose by trying to help him. I couldn't make it worse, could I?

He leaned forward. "Will you help me?"

I glanced at my grandpa. He knew what it was like to be suspected of a murder or two he hadn't committed. "What do you think, Grandpa? Will you help, too? You probably have more contacts that will be helpful than I do given when it was and the type of folks she was hanging around."

He shook his head. "Maggie May, this is not your problem to solve."

"I know that. But…"

"But you're going to try anyway."

I shrugged. "He asked for my help. And I believe him."

My grandpa reached for his non-existent pack of cigarettes. (He'd stopped smoking a few years before after a lifetime of two packs a day). "Fine. I'll help. But only to get to the bottom of this."

He turned back to Evan Browers. "I'm not as naïve as my granddaughter. I've seen men who could claim they were innocent and be believed while holding a bloody knife standing over a dead body. So if you did this, we'll prove that, too. Beyond the shadow of a doubt."

"I didn't."

"We'll see."

And with that, I was on another murder investigation. My cop husband was going to be so happy.

CHAPTER 6

I walked Evan Browers to the door and then returned to the kitchen. My grandpa hadn't moved an inch. And he did not look happy. "Maggie May."

"What?" I huffed out a breath and sat down next to him, grabbing another bite of fudge from the tray. I knew I was eating too much of it. (Of that and lasagna and all sorts of other comfort foods.) But it made me happy and if 2020 had taught me anything it was that I should let myself be happy while I could, because you never knew when a global catastrophe was going to come along and wipe all of that away.

As I debated making myself another cup of hot chocolate, my grandpa asked, "What are you thinking, telling that man you'll take on his case? You're not a private investigator."

"I know. But who else is going to help him?"

"A private investigator."

"You saw him, Grandpa. He needs help. And he asked me to be the person who does that." I crossed my arms and tried not to pout. "You know, I'm not bad at this."

"You want to be an investigator, become an investigator. But stop poking your nose into other people's business. One of these days someone is going to poke back at you."

I shook my head. "Doubtful. I mean, we're talking something that happened over thirty years ago. The person who did this—let's be real, the *man* who did this—is probably already dead. And if he isn't dead he's in prison somewhere for some other crime. Men who do these things don't usually stop at one. And if he isn't dead or in prison, he's probably old and infirm."

"Like me? Am I old and infirm?" He glared me down from across the table.

There was only one right answer to that question, but I was so tempted to answer the other way. "No."

"Well then."

I pressed my lips together, trying to figure out why I had taken the case. I didn't particularly like the man. Truth be told he was off in some way that made me uncomfortable. One of those people who doesn't quite know how to act normal so always gives people a weird vibe.

And while I did feel sorry for him, I didn't feel *that* sorry for him.

But…

"Look, Grandpa. If he didn't do this then that means there is someone who is part of this community who did. Or who is now part of another community who did. And I don't think it's right that someone can do that sort of thing to a woman and just get away with it and live happily ever after. It's not…fair."

I decided I did want that second cup of hot chocolate and went to make it. After I'd shoved the measuring cup of water in the microwave, I added, "That's not justice. It's not right. That someone can take a young girl's life and then live theirs with no consequences. And back then people weren't as aware of DNA and things like that. So whoever did this is far more likely to have messed up back then than they are now if they're still doing this sort of thing."

I tore open the chocolate powder packet and dumped it in the cup. "So, sure, maybe I'll stir something up I shouldn't. But someone has to. Because that girl was murdered and her killer wasn't caught. The tools didn't exist back then to catch him. But now they do. And we should use them. Every rapist and murderer tracked down and caught is a warning to every other man who thinks he can get away with something like that, that he can't and he'll be caught eventually. It makes every woman that much safer, including me."

"Some things are best left alone, Maggie May."

"Nope. Not this."

He shook his head. "Fine. But promise me you won't interview anyone dangerous without me or Matt there."

"Promise, Grandpa."

He pushed himself to his feet. "I'll let Lesley know, too. She might be able to find something at the library. Or know some of the gossip from back then. You want to come over for dinner tonight?"

"Better not. Matt had an early shift today so he'll actually be home for dinner. I want to fix him something special to soften him up before I ask for access to the case file."

My grandpa narrowed his eyes as he watched me eat yet another piece of fudge. He opened his mouth as if to say something, but didn't. Good thing, too, because my weight is no one's business but mine and I would've let him have it if he'd made any sort of comment.

So I'd put on a few pounds, who cared? No one else had to live in my body but me. And it turns out my body was happier full of fudge than not.

I walked him to the door and then turned to survey the living room where Fancy was snoring away against the wall, ignoring the wonderful, comfortable dog bed I'd just bought her.

I needed to do some internet research. And come up with a fancy meal idea to soften Matt up. No grilled cheese sandwiches for us tonight, no sirree.

Although that sounded really good. Maybe I could have one for a snack before he got home…Grilled cheese sandwich for second lunch and then steak and potatoes for dinner. Mmm.

Maybe I could do cream cheese mashed potatoes with some bacon in them to go with it. If that didn't make Matt my willing slave, I didn't know what would.

CHAPTER 7

Of course, before I could start investigating the murder, I had to meet with Jamie and Greta first. We were trying to run a business after all and we'd agreed to get together to share our latest ideas for the pet resort.

Jamie was in charge of the café for people, I was in charge of the bakery for dogs, Greta was in charge of choosing how to spend the money. It was mostly hers after all. But I could at least provide the place to meet (and the fudge).

Jamie arrived first. She was positively beaming with happiness and so pregnant I wondered how she could even walk with that big belly of hers. She'd cut her long brown hair into a cute bob that hit right at her chin making her look even more adorable than normal.

She gave me a quick hug and grabbed a bite of fudge before putting the ice cream samples she'd brought into the freezer.

"How's it going?" I asked. "The nursery ready yet?"

"No. I've had the nursery re-painted three times so far. I just want the perfect shade of yellow and none of them are quite right. They're either too bright or too pale or too…Ugh. *Green*."

"You know, I always figured I'd paint my nursery white with black geometric patterns along the top of the wall. Newborns can't tell colors anyway, but sharp lines and stuff are good for their eyes. So I've heard. I'd probably throw in some red shapes, too. Supposedly that's the first color they can see."

She looked at me like I'd grown two heads. "That's not soothing. Or restful. You would really paint a nursery black and white and red?"

"Yeah. I'm surprised more people don't. It's psychology after all."

Before she could say more, Greta arrived with Hans, her Irish Wolfhound. Fancy was thrilled to have the company, which she showed by sniffing him for a few seconds and then lying down nearby.

Greta gave us each kisses on the cheek and then set her fabric samples on the kitchen table. She was her usual polished self with her pale blonde hair pulled back into a chignon at the base of her neck and slim black slacks and a bright purple silk top.

"Jamie, you look wonderful. Maggie, you do as well. What have I missed?" she asked in that wonderful Germanic accent of hers that made everything sound more posh than it was.

"Oh, nothing much," I answered. "Jamie was just telling me she's repainted the nursery three times because she can't find the right shade of yellow."

"It's horrible. I think it's fine and then the sun comes up the next morning and it's too bright or too dull or too subtle." She sighed and sat down on the couch, propping her feet up on the coffee table with a wince.

Greta tsked. "This is why you do not paint the entire nursery. You put a small square. You then look at the square at different times of day. You see how it does." She grabbed her phone. "Here. Give me paper."

I handed her a notepad and pen and she scrawled a name and phone number on the page, her Ms looking more like Ws.

"This is my designer. Call her. She will tell you the proper yellow to use for a baby's bedroom."

Jamie tucked the piece of paper away in her oversized purse. "Thank you. Maggie said she's just going to paint her nursery white with black geometric shapes."

"Ah, so you are finally telling people. Congratulations."

"Congratulations on what?" I asked.

Greta glanced at my belly and back at my face. "On your pregnancy."

"I'm not pregnant. I've just gained a little weight and this type of top makes me look pregnant." Anything gathered below the chest that hangs loose has that effect.

"Hm. Are you sure?"

"Yes, I'm sure. I would know if I was pregnant."

Jamie and Greta exchanged a look.

"I would know."

"Hm. Of course. But you may want to check. Just in case."

"Change of subject, please. Jamie, what do you have planned for the delivery? Can the local hospital do it or are you going to have to go to Denver? If so, I hope there are protections in place to keep you safe."

We'd been happily living in our little bubble while the world around us got scarier, and I didn't relish the idea of Jamie having to leave to go to Denver. Especially to a hospital.

"Actually, I wanted to talk to you about that. I've decided I want to do a home birth. And since our entire house is wood floors, I was hoping we could do it here?" She winced a bit as she gave me that wide-eyed pleading look she'd used to such great effect on all of her past boyfriends.

I stared at her in horror. "A home birth? You're going to shove something the size of a football out of a place much smaller than a football and you would like to do that in my living room? I mean, yes, you are my best friend, but no. I do not need front row seats to *that*. Nnno."

It turned out there were in fact limits to my friendship. I'd kill someone for my best friend or help her bury the body if she needed me to, but I was not going to let her give birth in my living room.

"Wait, you aren't going to be there?" she asked.

"That's what Mason's for. And your mom. They were there at the various beginnings of things; they can be there for the culmination of this particular series of events. *I* will come by the next day when you are all tidied up, and I will bring a balloon and politely refuse to hold something so small and delicate lest I break it."

"It?"

"Well, I don't know the sex do I? Him, her. The child. Lest I break the child."

Greta patted Jamie on the hand as she sat down next to her. "You can have your baby at my house. I will arrange it."

"Are you sure, Greta?"

"Oh yes, my late husband, he was very concerned about his health. We have a full medical suite on the second floor. I will make sure that there is whatever is needed for a baby."

"I want a water birth, not some horrible thing involving stirrups."

"Yes, yes. Of course. We will arrange for that. We will have nice music and a warm pool of water. But the stirrups will also be there. Just in case. And a doctor."

"I was thinking of using a doula."

Greta patted her on the hand once more. "Hm. Yes, well. We will have both, no? Just to be safe."

As they continued to discuss the details of the birth, I stared back and forth at them in horror. These were the types of things people were just supposed to go off and do. No one who wasn't an intimate part of the situation needed to be privy to the actual details.

Just like I hadn't needed the details of the conception, I didn't need the details of the delivery.

"Alrighty, then," I finally interrupted. "Let's get this party started and see what Hans thinks of my latest treat invention, the Steak Sizzler."

Fancy immediately jumped to her feet when I opened the container. If possible, the Steak Sizzlers were her all-time favorite treat. Of course for a dog who would gleefully eat cardboard if it was given to her with enough enthusiasm, (I kid, she wouldn't, not really, I don't think) it was sometimes hard to tell the difference between normal "I will gobble this up" and extraordinary "I will gobble this up."

Hans was more considered in his approach, but once he came close enough to sniff the little steak bite I offered him, he too gobbled it up.

"Looks like we have another winner," I declared.

"Great. Time for ice cream." Jamie lumbered herself up from the couch and waddled into the kitchen, wincing a bit as she walked on her swollen feet.

I shuddered. I was definitely not ready for that, thank you very much. Me, pregnant? Ugh. Some thoughts were just too scary to contemplate.

As Jamie took her samples out of the freezer and I arranged for bowls and spoons, I instead thought about the murder of Mary Diever and what I'd need to do after this meeting to get started on the investigation.

Compared to the horrors of childbirth, that was downright pleasant.

CHAPTER 8

By the time Matt came home from work I had not only whipped up the mashed potatoes and loaded them down with sour cream and bacon, but I also had two juicy T-bone steaks ready to go in the broiler once the roasted Brussels sprouts were done. I'd also prepared a balsamic glaze I found on the internet that I hoped was going to make them so absurdly delicious you could cry.

Seriously, what did people do before they could find recipes online? Crazy to think about.

(And on top of the great recipe I'd also learned that Brussels sprouts hadn't always tasted as good as they do now. Turns out someone revived an old version of them because they'd become woefully bitter over the years. Who knew? The things you can learn from strangers. Hopefully that was actually true. I chose to believe so.)

"Hey, honey," I said as Matt came into the kitchen.

Man, was he beautiful. Six-foot. Dark hair. Blue eyes. And in uniform? Mm, yummy.

Of course, his physical looks had nothing on his heart of gold and his willingness to put up with my you-know-what. I had won the lottery marrying him. And for some crazy reason he thought he was the lucky one. Which, honestly, is how it should work in my opinion. Both people in the relationship should feel just the slightest bit lucky that this amazing person chose them.

And I was. No doubt about it.

He glanced around the kitchen and smiled. "Special occasion?"

"In a manner of speaking."

"Great. Let me get showered and then you can tell me the news."

He rushed off to the bathroom as my timer went off and I busied myself with swapping out the Brussels sprouts for the steaks.

Fifteen minutes later we settled in at the table. Matt smiled at me like a schoolboy. I swear, his eyes were twinkling as he grinned at me.

"Why do you look so happy?" I asked him.

"Well…" He raised his eyebrows like we shared some sort of secret.

"Well, what?"

"I mean, the meal. And you said it was a special occasion."

Had I?

I frowned. "Look, Matt, I'm not sure what you think this meal is about, but I'm pretty sure it's not about whatever it is you think it's about."

His smile dimmed. "It isn't?"

"No. I don't think so. I mean, I made this meal to butter you up so you wouldn't be mad at me." I slipped Fancy a little bit of my mashed potatoes so she'd stop drooling on the floor while she waited for us to start eating.

"Mad at you for what?" Matt asked suspiciously.

"We'll get to that in a minute. First, what did you think this meal was about?"

He crossed his arms and sat back. "Well, I mean...You know. I've been pretty patient. I wanted to give you your space, but I am your husband. And at some point...I mean, we're in this together, aren't we?"

I stared at him, baffled. "I have no idea what you're talking about. What do I need space for?" And then it dawned on me. "Oh not you, too! Matt, I am not pregnant. I have just gained a bit of weight. It's been one of those years. Look, sorry to disappoint, but I made a fancy meal because I didn't want you to be mad that I'm going to investigate another murder, okay? Sorry."

"What? Who? Where? There haven't been any murders around here lately."

I cut a bite off my steak, probably with a little more force than was necessary. "It's not a recent one. It was thirty-six years ago. Mary Diever."

He started cutting his steak just as aggressively. "Mary Diever? But we know who killed her. Evan Browers. We're just waiting on the DNA to prove it."

I rubbed the back of my neck and grimaced. "It's your case?"

"Yes. We got some special federal funding to DNA test old cases and the Chief assigned it to me. I thought I'd told you about it? Anyway. There was a witness that saw him near her house that morning, and we found his t-shirt about a hundred feet from the murder scene. A pretty distinctive one. Even back then everyone knew it was him, but it was all circumstantial so they never arrested him. Give it a week or two, though, and we'll have the DNA to back it up."

He speared a Brussels sprout on his fork. "Why do you suddenly want to investigate this case anyway?"

I bit my lip. "Because Evan Browers asked me to?"

"When?"

"Today. When I took Fancy for a walk." I forced myself not to chew on my thumbnail as I waited for Matt's reaction.

He carefully set down his fork and knife and stared at me very intently. "Evan Browers approached you when you were out alone on a walk?"

"It wasn't like that." I mean, it was, but I wasn't going to tell him that now that I'd decided Evan Browers wasn't a bad guy. "He asked for my help because he thinks you guys won't believe him."

"If he's innocent the DNA will show that. You don't need to get involved."

I wrinkled my nose. "Actually…I'm pretty sure the DNA's not gonna help his case."

"And why's that?" he asked, his voice going flat.

I slipped Fancy a few bites of steak onto her sharing plate before I answered. "Because he told me they were involved? They used to meet in a little spot right by where her body was found. And they'd been together that morning. But she was alive when he left."

Matt sat back, shaking his head in disbelief. "He told you they were involved."

I nodded.

"Then why didn't he tell the police that?"

"Because he didn't think it would help. He thought it would make him look more like the killer. And I'm not sure he's wrong about that. I mean, lying to the police is bad, but sometimes telling the police the whole truth can turn out poorly, too."

Lord knows I'd seen that a time or two.

Matt shoved his plate away, his steak half-eaten.

"Aren't you going to finish that?" I asked.

"Somehow I've lost my appetite."

I frowned at him. Matt is normally a really decent guy, but he has his moments. Everyone does.

"Don't be like that, Matt. The man asked me for help and after I talked to him—with my grandpa present, I might add—I decided I believed him so I'd try to help. I didn't know it was your case. And I had nothing to do with him not telling you the full truth about his relationship with Mary Diever. So, please, eat your steak and I'll tell you everything I know. If it's any consolation, Grandpa thinks he's guilty, too. Maybe we'll find something to strengthen your case for you instead of ruin it."

He frowned off into space, but didn't immediately reach for his plate.

"Plus, if you don't eat that steak, I probably will. And since I've gained so much weight everyone thinks I'm pregnant, I probably don't need to do that."

That got his attention. "You really don't think you are?"

"No! Of course not. I mean it's my body, don't you think I'd notice if I was growing a child inside me?"

"Normally I'd say yes, but…are you sure?"

"Matt!"

"How about you take a test, just to be on the safe side. You don't want to end up on an episode of that show about women who didn't know they were pregnant until it came time to deliver do you?"

I rolled my eyes. "Fine. I will pick up a test at the store next time I'm there. It's going to be negative, though. I am not pregnant. Now, about this murder…"

CHAPTER 9

The next day I dropped in on Lesley at the library where she still volunteered twice a week.

She's a lovely woman, but she's always so put together it makes me feel like there has to be a stain somewhere on my clothes even when there isn't. She'd recently cut her hair and was sporting a look that framed her face with soft snow-white curls that curved around her chin. It looked good on her.

Of course, she was one of those people who always look good. Nice clothes, nice tasteful jewelry, and old but still beautiful.

My grandpa was a lucky man to have found a second chance with her. Not that it had been easy to accept when he did, because it was hard to see him replace my grandma, but he deserved happiness and Lesley gave him that.

"Hey, Lesley, how are you?" I asked as I walked over to where she sat behind the circulation desk.

It was still weird to me to walk into the "new" library with all its wide open space and computers and meeting rooms. I'd always have a special place in my heart for the old library that had been an interconnected warren of rooms on the top floor of the court building. That was the library of my childhood summers.

"I'm good, Maggie. Your grandpa told me about the Mary Diever investigation. Looking into another murder are you?"

"That I am. He thought you might know something? Or be able to find some old records?"

"Well, I did make some calls this morning so let me fill you in on what I found out." She pulled a small notebook out from under the counter and scanned through her notes. I couldn't read them. They must've been in shorthand.

She sighed and shook her head. "A tragic story all around. Mary was an only child. Her mother passed away when she was about ten. Official word was that she died in her sleep, but she was a young woman. Thirty-five. Unofficial word was that she might have had other issues that contributed. Alcohol or pills. Mother's little helper of some sort. She wasn't from here and didn't really have any close friends, though, so no push to investigate."

"How'd she end up here if she wasn't from here originally?"

She glanced at her notepad. "Met Roger Diever when he was in law school in Philadelphia. When he came back to take over his father's law practice, she came with him. But she didn't join any committees or participate in any school activities. Kept to herself. Same for Mary."

"That's odd, isn't it?"

The Baker Valley was a small community and it seemed that everyone had been a scout of some sort or other or participated in the annual 4th of July parade or played on the co-ed t-ball team at some point in time.

"Perhaps. The women I spoke to assumed she didn't want to lower herself to associate with them. She was supposed to be from high society. As for Mary, they said the mother kept her away, too."

I pursed my lips. "Was she really that high-class? I mean, she lived here."

"Not a lot of lawyers and doctors in the area, that's for sure. And most people around here didn't go to college. To some people that matters."

I shook my head. Some people are fools. To think the degree on the wall matters more than the intelligence between the ears.

"What about Roger Diever?" I asked. "What did you learn about him?"

"From what I gathered, Roger Diever was a ruthless attorney who'd do almost anything to win. And even though he took over his father's practice, most of his legal work involved Denver clients."

"So why come back here? Why not move to Denver?"

"I presume it was his father. I didn't know the man well, but we did cross paths when I was younger. *He* was cold. Gave me the shivers. Also, not a man to accept anything other than getting his own way. I still remember when he set his sights on my friend, Doreen. It was like a military campaign for him. He lost a few of the battles, but he kept adjusting his strategy until she finally gave in and dated him. And then he dumped her two weeks later for a new target because he'd won."

Sounded like a charmer. Glad I'd never met him.

"Are either of them still alive?" I asked.

"No. They both died shortly after Mary did, actually. Mary's grandfather died about a month later. Brakes failed and he rolled his car off of Elk Road. Mary's father died about a year after that. Heart attack. Some said it was her death that broke him, especially after having already lost his wife. But there were rumors it was helped along by alcohol."

I winced. "What a tragic family history."

"Some families are like that, aren't they?"

Thinking back on my own losses, I nodded. It's like you let in one tragic, unexpected event and more shove their way in after. I just hoped my particular run of bad luck was finally over.

"Did you find anything else out? Any names of friends she had? Anything like that?"

She shook her head. "From everything I could find out, she really didn't have friends. No clubs. No sports. Nothing. Just her family and her studies."

I drummed my fingers on the countertop. This was not going to be an easy investigation. I sure hoped Matt's police file had something more for us to go on or I wasn't going to be able to help Evan Browers after all.

"What about partying? Mr. Browers mentioned she was maybe experimenting a bit with drugs."

"If she was, it wasn't with anyone local. At least not as far as anyone Lou talked to knew. Maybe she was hanging around with folks from out of town. This area wasn't the tourist destination back then that it is now, but there were definitely people who came here for a fun time for a week or a weekend and then left. If she was socializing with them, no one local would know."

I nodded. Made sense. Especially since most of the

people who'd come to the valley on vacation would have more money than the locals, so would be more "acceptable" for her to hang out with.

Of course, if something had happened with one of them, thirty-six years later who would remember some random guy who passed through town for a few days?

I sighed. "Alright. Thank you, Lesley. I appreciate it."

"You're welcome. I hope you can help Evan. I remember when he was just a little kid. Wasn't much of one for big books, but he liked the comic books. He'd come once a week and read them in the corner." She smiled at the memory. "If it's any consolation, I don't think he did this, so anything I can do to help, you just let me know."

"Will do. Thank you." I gave her a quick hug. "I better get going. I need to run by the grocery store before dinner tonight. Matt promised me he'd try to bring home the case file for us to look through."

Lesley shook her head. "I can't imagine sitting down at the kitchen table and discussing a murder with my husband, but to each their own."

I just smiled. Matt was perfect for me in so many ways, that one included.

CHAPTER 10

That night Matt brought home *two* legal boxes full of notes and photos, both from the original investigation and his follow-up. Fortunately, when he'd told the Chief that I wanted to see the files, the Chief had actually okayed it.

Seems I'd done a good enough job helping them out in the past that he was willing to give me that little bit of latitude.

As I reached for the lid on the first box, Matt moved it away. "Uh-uh. Pregnancy test first."

I rolled my eyes and crossed my arms. "I'm not pregnant."

"Good. Then you can go pee on a stick and we'll know for sure and then we can settle in for the night with a nice cozy cold case file."

"Can't I take the test after we look through the files?" I reached for the box again, but he moved it away once more. "No."

I narrowed my eyes at him. "Let me ask you something. How long have you thought I was pregnant?"

"A week or two. Maybe more."

"And yet not once did you mention it. Even though I drink a ton of Coke and beer and I probably eat things that I shouldn't if I really am pregnant."

"You may not have realized it, Maggie, but you kind of haven't been drinking beer at all. And you've cut way back on the Coke. And you're eating vegetables."

"What does that mean? *I'm eating vegetables.* I always eat vegetables with dinner."

He raised an eyebrow. "But do you normally randomly snack on vegetable trays throughout the day?"

I frowned at him. Just because I'd bought a veggie tray at the grocery store the last couple of times I was there didn't mean anything.

Although, he was right. I had munched on them throughout the day, which was not exactly normal for me. (Of course, that was in addition to everything else I'd munched on throughout the day.)

I shook my head. "That was just from going on the birth control. It makes me crave vegetables. Same thing happened in college."

"And when exactly did that happen? You going on birth control?"

I frowned at him, like how could he not remember. "Right after we got married."

"We went into lockdown right after we got married."

"Yeah. But…" I stopped and thought about it for a long moment.

I'd made the appointment, I remembered that.

But then everything shut down…And they told me I'd have to reschedule…But they didn't know when, so I couldn't…

And I was going to call them back…

But then I got distracted with my grandpa and his friends deciding to blow up part of the canyon to keep us all safe and isolated from stupid people who wanted to treat lockdown like a road trip vacation permission slip.

And…

I stared at Matt in horror. I'd never actually made the appointment.

How could I forget that?

"Oh no."

He nodded. "Wanna pee on that stick now?"

"Why didn't you say anything?"

He shrugged. "You knew I wanted to have kids as soon as possible. I just figured you'd changed your mind and wanted to, too. Or were going to leave it up to fate. I've heard you mention often enough how hard it was for some of your friends to conceive, and you are in that age range."

If Matt hadn't been Matt I wouldn't have trusted his explanation. But I suspected that's exactly what had happened. He'd just shrugged it off as no big deal. Let me be in charge of the entire direction of our lives without so much as a worry.

I grabbed the box and raced to the bathroom, suddenly desperate to know whether I really was pregnant or not.

All I can say about what happened next is it's a good thing they give you more than one of those things, because I didn't quite pull it off correctly the first time around. What can I say, I'd never had to do one of those before. (Never expected to ever do one, to be honest.)

And they're not exactly straight-forward. At least not the brand I bought, which was not the one with the cute baby on the box. It was the one that promised fast and accurate results. You know, for the woman freaking out that she might be unexpectedly pregnant.

Anyway.

Ten minutes later, after the peeing and the crying and the hyperventilating, I walked back into the living room where Matt was sprawled on the couch, a beer in hand, Fancy snoring at his feet.

"Well?" he asked.

I handed him the stick, my hand trembling.

He looked at it and let out a big whoop. "Yes! We're going to have a baby!" He jumped up from the couch, picked me up, and spun me around, startling Fancy into a barking fit.

Fortunately, his enthusiasm was contagious, because inside I was freaking the frick out. I was not ready to be pregnant.

There are women—Jamie is one of them—who have been talking about wanting to be mothers and how many kids they'll have since high school. *I* was not that girl. I was *never* that girl. Marriage, babies, they weren't exactly on the priority list.

Oh sure, I figured they'd happen someday. I wasn't opposed to the idea. Not a hundred percent. But maybe sixty percent. And whatever day I'd expected them to happen it was a day far in the future.

As much as I loved Matt, the whole marriage thing had been enough of a shock to the system, I wasn't exactly ready to go plunging into the next "this is how life works" stage.

Honestly, I'd kind of been planning to spend a decade or so married and then go, "Oh, golly gee, those eggs are all gone, so sorry" and live a happy life of quiet peace with just Matt, me, and Fancy.

But it seemed life was determined to shove me into that traditional path whether I was ready for it or not. And don't get me wrong, I knew I'd love the kid to pieces just like I loved Fancy to pieces. That was never in question. It was just…holy shit scary.

And yes, I just cussed. But, it was a cussable moment if there ever was one. I was pregnant.

Holy #@&!

CHAPTER 11

In my opinion the best thing to do when you find out that you are unexpectedly pregnant is to read an old murder case file and try not to think about it.

Matt on the other hand wanted to talk about our plans and whether we should buy our current house, which I didn't really like because it had stairs, or move elsewhere.

The house was conveniently located next door to my grandpa who I had moved to Creek to look after. But he didn't really need the help. Then again, maybe he and Lesley could help us with the kid. More Lesley, I assumed, since she'd actually raised kids whereas my grandpa had entered the picture after my dad was grown.

The other option, of course, was to move. But then the question was where to. Not like there were a lot of homes for sale in the area.

And if we were going to move that put Bakerstown on the table because we could be close to the pet resort and the auxiliary police station, which might even mean a promotion for Matt and would certainly make for an easier commute, especially in the winter.

So there were good reasons to stay and good reasons to go. But I had to finally, gently, tell Matt to please, shut, up. I was a little overwhelmed by the news and if he didn't want me to start hyperventilating into a paper sack we needed to leave that discussion for another day.

"Maggie, you do understand that we only have so long before that kid is here and the next five years of our life become a whirlwind, don't you?"

I reached for the crime scene photos, refusing to look at him. "I'm trying very hard not to think about that, thank you very much."

He laughed and I looked up in time to see him grinning at me, flashing the dimple in his cheek that only makes an appearance when he's really, really happy. "I can't believe we're going to be parents. I'm so excited. When should we tell everyone?"

Never probably wasn't an option, so instead I said, "Not yet. Not until after I know how far along I am."

(And could confirm this turn of events with a more reliable test than one that depended on my ability to properly use that stupid stick correctly.)

As I reached for another file out of the case boxes, Matt asked, "What do you want to name her? Or him? I guess it could be a boy, but I kind of hope this first one is a girl."

First one? Wasn't he getting a little ahead of things?

I shook my head. "Sorry, but we are not naming the baby until it's born."

"Can't we at least put together a shortlist?"

"No."

"Why not?"

Ah, this poor man. He did not know what he had married.

"Because things go wrong in life. And while I don't personally have some huge, strong belief in a higher power that takes a direct interest in my life, I do have this weird belief in fate and luck and jinxes. So we will not be naming this child until he or she is in our arms alive and well."

He looked at me with a sad understanding, but just gave me a kiss on the forehead. "Okay." But then that grin came back. "This is going to be such a fun adventure. I'm so happy."

"Right. Now, if you really are my loving, adoring husband who is going to support me through this mess, you will drop the subject of babies and futures and everything that's coming our way like a freight train, and will instead sit down and help me look through this case file for any clues as to who could've done this to Mary Diever." I flashed one of the crime scene photos at him.

As he took it he asked, "Other than Evan Browers?"

"Yes. Other than Evan Browers."

"Fine. But I won't promise not to think of baby names while I'm doing so."

I sighed. "Fine. Just don't share them with me, please."

🐾 🐾 🐾

An hour later we'd looked through the whole case file. It was not good. At least, not for Evan Browers. There were no notes about Mary's friends or another love interest. There was an investigative note that she'd had sex shortly before she was killed, but the autopsy report was missing entirely.

From the photos it was pretty clear she'd been bashed in the head with a rock, but if they'd found it, there was no record in the file. And no other obvious signs of trauma other than that, so chances were the DNA was going to only tie back to Evan Browers.

Also, as Matt had already mentioned, there was a witness who'd seen Evan Browers coming out of the woods that morning near where everything happened.

I sat back and frowned at the table. How do you prove that someone didn't kill someone thirty-six years ago when there's nothing to go on?

"Right. So. What are the angles?" I grabbed my notepad and started jotting down ideas.

"What about the father or grandfather," Matt suggested. "Either one could've discovered what she was doing with Evan that morning. There's a fight, it gets heated, and bam, she's dead."

"Could explain the tragedy of the next year, too. Grandfather kills her, father finds out and cuts his brakes, and then drinks himself to death." I wrinkled my nose. "Of course, that's a little too pat don't you think?"

I went to the fridge to grab more fudge, and then remembered I'd already eaten all of it the day before. Easy enough to make more. The recipe only required about 90 seconds in the microwave and then some time in the fridge. But I hesitated. Was I allowed fudge anymore? It was peanut butter not chocolate, but still.

Luckily I'd cut way back on the Coke because I'd been feeling a lot of indigestion. (I can't believe I hadn't noticed all the little signs of pregnancy before that…There were so many once I thought back on it.) But what about sweets in general? And weren't there certain cheeses I wasn't allowed to eat, too? And something about tuna fish maybe? And folic acid?

Jamie would know. She probably had a frickin' meal plan I could borrow. But if I told her she'd get all excited and I just couldn't do that yet.

"Who else?" I asked as I grabbed an apple from the fridge instead. I was pretty sure I'd never heard anyone say pregnant people can't have apples. "Someone in from out of town?" I added that to the list.

Matt nodded. "What about a drug dealer? If she really was doing drugs she might've gone direct to get them."

"Yep. Or what about a complete random stranger who just happened upon her in the woods, but didn't sexually assault her?"

He gave me a skeptical look.

"Yeah, I know. Not likely. But better to throw the net wide and narrow it down from there, right?"

"Well if you're going to do that, was there a money motive? Someone who wanted to inherit and took out the whole family?"

I wrote it down, but it also didn't seem likely.

"What about jealousy or lust?" I asked. "Those are always classics. Maybe she had a stalker. Or Evan Browers had someone he'd broken up with who was jealous he'd moved on. Maybe she had an ex who didn't take it well. Or another guy she was seeing, too."

He nodded. "It's easy to assume it's a man in these situations, but it doesn't have to be. Could easily be a woman, especially since it doesn't look like there was a sexual component."

"Right." I scrawled woman on my notepad to remind me not to assume it was a man, but I still believed it was a man. "What else? What other reasons do people have to kill someone?" I asked.

"Power."

"How would power play into it? She was a college student."

He shrugged. "I don't know."

I wrote it down at the bottom of the list. Just because I couldn't think of anything right now didn't mean I wouldn't later as I learned more about her and her life.

I glanced at the two boxes once more. "No offense, but I wish the original investigators had done more work than they did."

"If you're going to blame them, you have to blame me, too. I didn't do much more."

"I wasn't trying to criticize you, Matt, I promise."

He held up his hand. "No, it's a fair assessment. As a new investigator I have to constantly remind myself not to jump to conclusions about who is guilty. It's too easy to fixate on an obvious suspect and be blinded to the other possibilities. Of course, it doesn't help that outside of books and movies and real crime shows that a lot of murders really are that obvious. It usually *is* the husband or boyfriend."

"And, see, since all of my experience is from watching shows and movies, I'm pre-conditioned to look for some twisty motive when in real life it's usually just Person A knew Person B really well and something made them decide to kill them. Like a huge life insurance policy."

I wrote that down.

"Exactly." He glanced at the notepad and then at me. "So are we done? Can we eat and talk about babies now?"

I flinched. "Do not say that."

"Say what?"

"Babies. As in plural. Twins run in my family, Matt. At least on my dad's side they do. Maybe. My dad was an only child and his dad only had brothers, but the two or three generations above that? All had twins."

He grinned. "Really? So maybe we could have a boy and a girl right from the start?"

"Matt!"

"What?"

"No."

"Maggie, it's too late. If you're having twins, you're having twins. Which would be great, wouldn't it? That means we could maybe have six kids before you get too old for more."

"Six kids?" I curled up in horror. "See, this is why you date someone for years before you marry them. So you know that they want six kids and you can say no, sorry, you better find someone else."

"Would you have really told me that? Is six kids a deal-breaker?" He mooned at me with those gorgeous blue eyes of his, but I wasn't having it.

"Yes! Six kids is a deal-breaker."

"What about three?"

"Can we just get through one? I have more than one friend who had that first kid or, more often, that second kid, and was like, oh hey, I'm good. No more. So let's see where we're at after this first…one."

He grinned again. "Twins."

"Shut up. We don't know that yet."

"But, maybe…"

As he went to the kitchen to whip something up for dinner my mind started to cycle through everything I was going to have to take care of before the kid or kids were born. It was not a short list. And I did not have the time to get it all done.

Which meant by all rights I should call Evan Browers up and tell him I couldn't help right now. But I'd promised. And if I didn't help he was very likely going to be in jail by the time I gave birth.

Plus, I was enough of an independent woman that if I hadn't had a murder or crime to investigate I would've probably gone out looking for one just to prove to myself that I was not going to let motherhood consume me. Which meant it was good, actually, that I had a case to solve. One less thing to put on the to-do list.

Now if I just had a snowball's chance in you-know-where of actually solving it. That would help.

CHAPTER 12

The next morning as I stood in my kitchen and tried to figure out what to make for breakfast, I realized I had two choices: I could call up Jamie who probably had a pregnancy meal planner that optimized for nutrition at each stage of pregnancy and ask her what I was allowed to eat, or I could wade into the realms of pregnancy forums and websites to figure it out for myself.

Since I didn't want to accidentally go down some weird pregnancy conspiracy theory black hole, I decided Jamie was the safer option. Not that her whole home birth idea was something I was on-board with, so I'd approach it with a bit of skepticism still, but I'd known her for years and found her generally intelligent and level-headed.

Far better getting my information from her than listening to some rando who believed who-knows-what. (The internet is a blessing and a curse. As nice as it is to find information at your fingertips, sometimes that information has absolutely no connection to reality.)

Of course, that meant telling her I was pregnant. And I just...I wasn't quite ready for other people to be happy about my being pregnant. I know, that's weird. Everyone wants you to believe that being pregnant is this wonderful, glorious, life-affirming process that any woman should want to rush into head first and with bells on.

But it's actually *a lot*.

It's hormonal changes and physical changes and lifestyle changes. And not all of those changes are good ones. Maybe it was my worst-case-scenario brain working on overdrive, but I'd noticed those formerly-pregnant women on the "I have a weird medical issue" shows where things were not right after the fact, you know? Birth is a violent act.

And because I hadn't planned it, I was having horrid thoughts about birth defects and what does folic acid even do and should I be shoving handfuls of it in my mouth now to make up for not taking it in the months before I got pregnant.

To calm myself down I turned my attention to the murder investigation. Maybe Jamie's husband, Mason Maxwell, would know more about the family. He was rich. And a lawyer.

He answered on the second ring.

"Mason Maxwell, Esquire, how can I help you?"

Seriously? He said the esquire part? Who does that?

"Mason, it's Maggie. How are you?"

Fancy, noticing that I was on the phone and thus vulnerable to her antics, started crying until I slipped her a few steak sizzlers.

"I am doing well, Maggie. Surprised to hear from you, though, on my business line."

Even though he was married to my best friend and I'd come to accept him, I'd never come to adore him. He was just a little stick up the you-know-what for me. But he was a very handsome (older) man who had more than enough money to provide a good life for my friend and her child, and he treated her right, which was really the most important thing. It was clear he adored her and for that I was willing to forgive the fact that he seemed to not understand how to use contractions.

I left Fancy in the kitchen before she could start crying at me again. "I know. I'm not much of one for random social calls. So let me get right to the point. I'm investigating a murder and thought you could help with some background information."

"A murder? Whose?"

"Mary Diever. My understanding is her father and her grandfather were lawyers and she'd just returned home from her first year at college when she was killed."

"That was a long time ago."

"Thirty-six years."

"And why are you investigating it now?"

I settled in upstairs where I knew Fancy wouldn't follow me, although I could hear her crying from downstairs. "Evan Browers asked me to. The police took his DNA and he thinks they'll arrest him when it comes back, but he said he didn't kill her."

"Why would there be a DNA match then?"

"They were involved."

"Interesting. That does explain a few things."

"How so?"

"As you probably surmised, Mary's family and my own moved in similar social circles. Her father and grandfather both belonged to the country club and would golf on occasion. That summer, when Mary returned from school, her father tried to set us up."

Interesting.

"And?"

"I was willing. She was an attractive young woman, good family, similar backgrounds. There were synergies there. But she was not. I asked her to join me for lunch at the club, but she refused. Same with playing tennis or golfing. I thought maybe we could chat casually at the Fourth of July party, but she was not in attendance."

"Did you see any signs she was a drinker? Or into drugs? Or maybe was more friendly towards others at the club who were, um…a little more…?"

"Were a little more fun?" he asked, with a slight chuckle in his voice.

"Uh, yeah, that."

He thought about it for a moment. "No. There weren't many of us around that were that age and of that," he cleared his throat softly, "social standing. As far as I know she stayed away from all of us. Most of her time was spent at home."

"And what about the father? Or the grandfather? What did you know about them?"

"A little before my time. I was just getting started in practice when they both died. I know my father was not sorry to see either one of them go. I was not privy to the details but there was a case where my father was on one side and her grandfather was on the other. My father believed her grandfather had violated his duty in some way, perhaps by letting a client perjure himself on the stand to win. It was never clear to me what exactly had happened only that my father did not approve."

"And yet they would've been okay with you marrying Mary?"

"My family? No. It was her father and grandfather who wanted the match. Their family had been in the valley two generations but were still considered outsiders. Mary marrying me would have solved that. Well, at least for our children."

I thought about what that meant for Jamie's child or children. Would they associate with my little brat or brats or would we be too far beneath them? I knew Jamie. She'd never cut me off. But for kids it's hard. Life forces them to choose and in the ugliest ways possible. It's like a little Lord of the Flies at every middle school.

"Alright, so, they wanted social standing. But then I don't understand why the women kept themselves apart the way they did."

Mason was silent.

"Mason? Do you know something?"

"I am not one to gossip."

"Look, I'm trying to clear a man's name in a thirty-six-year-old homicide. If you know something, please share it. It could be the difference between his going to prison for life and his being able to live out the rest of his years as a free man. Please, Mason, tell me what you know even if it's conjecture."

He inhaled deeply. "Very well. My mother made a comment once. She stopped by their house to visit, because my mother will recruit anyone to her pet causes, and she at least did not believe that Mary's mother was too far above her."

"What was the comment?"

"That in her experience women who wear long sleeves in the middle of summer usually have something to hide. Obviously there was more to it than her choice of attire, but it was my mother's way of saying she suspected Mrs. Diever was being abused. It was never proven as far as I know. And if the rumors about her alcoholism were true, then that could have just as easily been the cause of any bruises she was trying to hide."

"But you don't think it was alcohol abuse? Having heard about her husband?"

"I do not know and could not give any testimony related to the matter."

I laughed softly. "You're such a lawyer sometimes, Mason."

"Thank you. I take that as a compliment."

I shook my head. I could never be married to Mason Maxwell. But to each their own. Jamie was happy and that's what mattered. "Alright, thank you for the information. If you think of anything else, please let me know."

"My pleasure."

"Also, is Jamie around today, do you know?"

"She just stepped into my office. Do you want to talk to her? I can give her the phone. I have to join a Zoom meeting in a moment anyway."

"Um, yeah, that would be great, thanks."

As I waited for Jamie to pick up the phone, I glanced down the stairs to where Fancy had settled herself, watching and waiting for me to come back downstairs. She wasn't crying anymore, but she was not resting either. That silly dog…

"Hey, Maggie, how are you?" Jamie asked.

I closed my eyes. I was dreading this conversation, but I figured it's like pulling off a Band-Aid, you just have to get it done as fast as possible and try not to scream when it hurts.

CHAPTER 13

Where to start when you have to tell your best friend you're pregnant...

"I'm good, but um...I could use your help." I paced down the hallway, wincing at what was going to come next.

"Sure, what with?"

"I, um, I'm, uh..."

"Oh! Did you finally take a pregnancy test? You're pregnant aren't you?" She didn't have to sound so excited about it.

"How did you know?" I stopped and glared at the wall, exasperated. Was I the only one who hadn't known?

"What else would it be? I've been waiting for this call every single day for the last month or two."

"Month or two? I've probably only been pregnant for a couple of weeks. Or like six weeks if you factor in the first month that doesn't really count."

"Oh, Maggie, no. It's been longer than that."

I sank to the floor. "Don't tell me that. I didn't take folic acid. I didn't eat the right things. I probably ate things that were bad for me. Like cheese. I love cheese, Jamie. I eat it every single day."

"But you don't eat fancy cheese every single day. You're fine. Look, if I'd seen you eating something that was truly terrible for the baby I would've probably said something."

"I've had beer. And Coke."

"It's fine. You're fine. Look, let me give you the number of my doctor. She's great and she promised me she'd squeeze you in as soon as you called. And I'll email you over my meal lists."

"I knew you'd have those." I rested my head against the wall, part of me relieved that she'd gone through this before me so she could help and part of me panicked that I was maybe further along than I'd thought.

"I'll also include my own personal list of what to expect so you can prepare. Are you still going to paint the baby's room white with black patterns on the walls now that you know you're actually pregnant?"

"I don't know, maybe. Although, there is some weird instinct that has me suddenly thinking about soothing pastels. But there really are psychological studies behind the black and white thing. Plus, I probably won't know the gender until the baby is born. And white will make the room much easier to use later."

Jamie laughed. "Use later? Like when the kid goes off to college?"

I sighed, the reality of what was happening finally hitting me smack in the face. "Oh no. This is eighteen years of my life growing in my belly."

"Eighteen years?" Jamie laughed again. "No, this is the rest of your life. Unless something really goes wrong somewhere down the line."

"Great, thanks. That really helped. I think I'm going

to go put my head in the toilet and cry."

"Don't be silly, Maggie. Eat a Saltine for the nausea. I've had a few friends who only felt fine if they were snacking all day long."

"Hm. Maybe that explains my current fascination with peanut butter fudge…"

"Probably. I'll send over the lists right now. I'm so happy! We get to raise our kids together."

I let out a deep breath. "That is the silver lining to all of this. Although, I was kind of hoping for the free babysitting. You know, let you get about four years ahead."

"Nope. Sorry. We're going to bumble through this together. It'll be good, Maggie, I promise."

"I hope you're right."

"I am. You'll come around, don't worry."

After I hung up the phone, I stared at the ceiling. How? How had my life so drastically transformed in such a short period of time? All I'd wanted to do was move to small-town Colorado and open a little business with my best friend.

But now, marriage? And kids? And the business had morphed into something so much bigger than my little cheesy idea…What was all this mess?

I went to the kitchen and opened the fridge. At least I now had an excuse for eating my feelings. Good thing there was still some lasagna leftover from the other day.

Fancy had followed me to see what I was up to, since she knows she always gets a little bit of whatever I eat. She crowded closer as I peeled back the cellophane. I sniffed at the lasagna to see if it was still good and Fancy's eyes widened in horror. She immediately ran out the doggie door and disappeared outside.

I shook my head as I searched for a fork. I had the weirdest dog. I could inhale deeply and she was fine with it. But one little double sniff and she went into immediate panic mode and had to leave the room.

What traumatic moment in her past had brought that on? It was probably something I'd done.

As I poked violently at the lasagna I thought about how if I could turn a sweet, adorable dog into a neurotic mess that was scared of the sound of sniffing, what damage was I going to do to a living, breathing child who could actually understand what I said?

Oh, dear.

Matt could save for our kid's college fund. I was going to save for their therapy fund. Because with me as mom, that kid was going to need it.

Mom.

Me. Holy…I shuddered and shoved more lasagna into my mouth.

Murder. Better to focus on murder.

CHAPTER 14

I decided the first thing I needed to do was track down the autopsy report. Assuming there was one. Small town, thirty-six years ago, there were no guarantees. But my grandpa would know who at least had been in charge of that sort of thing. And if he didn't, Lesley would.

I leashed up Fancy and we strolled next door. Even though I knew the front door would be unlocked, I still knocked. I don't care how old they are, a newly-married couple is not to be walked in on without permission.

Lesley answered the door wearing the cutest embroidered apron I'd ever seen. (Then again, it's quite possible it was the only embroidered apron I'd ever seen, but it was still cute.) It had prancing reindeer along the border with a jolly Santa in the middle.

"Baking?" I asked as the smell of warm sugar and pumpkin filled my nose.

"You guessed it." She stepped back so I could follow her inside.

"It smells delicious. What is that?"

"Pumpkin bread. And after that some pumpkin cookies. I'm visiting my daughter tomorrow and wanted to make sure I brought along enough goodies for the grandkids. Plus it gets me in the holiday spirit. You and Matt are coming over for Thanksgiving?"

"I think that's the plan. You're okay with Jack and Trish and Sam coming, too, right?" We were lucky to be walled off from the insanity of the rest of the world so we could safely gather.

"Absolutely."

I rubbed carefully at my back, trying not to make it obvious. How had I gone from not realizing I was pregnant to wanting to be off my swollen feet in a day? Probably psychosomatic.

Lesley gave me a shrewd look. "It was the worst with my first one. The back pain."

"I...You knew I was pregnant, too?" I asked.

"You didn't?"

I shook my head. "Not until Matt forced me to take a test yesterday. Here I am, priding myself on solving these various mysteries that have come my way over the last year and a half, and I somehow missed the fact that I was pregnant."

She smiled. "The mind's a funny thing. Come on. Have a seat in the kitchen and I'll get you some tea and a slice of pumpkin bread."

"Am I okay eating that?"

She patted my shoulder. "Yes, you'll be fine. Plus, remember, when I was having kids none of us knew all these rules and for the most part it turned out fine. You're not a closet alcoholic or drug addict are you?"

"No!"

"Well, then, you're probably just fine." She bustled around, preparing the tea and bread for me as I sat down at the kitchen table.

"I'm scared," I told her. My mom and grandma were gone, which made Lesley the closest thing I had to a mom.

She nodded in understanding as she settled into the chair across from me. "And you should be. It's a big change. To your body, to your life. I loved being a mother, every minute of it from poopy diapers and colic to first grade musicals and high school graduations. But that doesn't mean it was easy. Or that it didn't change my life in ways I'd never anticipated. And you're one for using that mind of yours. I'd expect nothing less than a bit of panic."

I took a bite of the bread and mmm'ed in pleasure. It was delicious. "Twins run in my family, you know."

"Ah, that would add an extra level of concern, wouldn't it?" She squeezed my hand. "Don't worry. We'll be here to help."

"What if we move? Matt thinks we should move to Bakerstown. And I really don't like our house, but I do like being near you guys."

"We'll still come by to babysit when you need it, even if you move. Maybe not quite as often. But you won't be alone with this, Maggie. We'll be there. Now, is that why you came by? To tell us?"

I cringed. "No, actually, I was going to wait until I saw the doctor to confirm it. I was still kind of hoping it was a false positive. I know that's horrible, but I just wasn't quite ready for this."

"If you waited to be ready, you'd never do anything in life that's worth doing. Or so the old saying goes."

"True. I guess. I did sort of jump into owning Fancy and marrying Matt and both of those have turned out alright so far."

"See, there you go. Now. The reason for your visit."

I finished the last of my pumpkin bread before answering. "I'm wondering if you know who the medical examiner was thirty-six years ago? Or if there wasn't one, who would've looked at Mary Diever's body?"

"There's no record of it in the file?"

I shook my head. "I know they probably didn't have someone fulltime to do that sort of thing, but no mention of it at all."

"Hm. Maybe check with the lead investigator on the case. Who was that?" She put another slice of bread on my plate. I would've felt guilty for eating up her bread, but there were six loaves cooling on the counter.

"Adam Ripley." I took another bite of bread, savoring all the yummy spices, and slipped Fancy a little bit, too.

"Oh, Adam. Nice man. He's retired now. Has been for quite some time. But still comes into the library every couple of weeks. We have a nice chat when he does. He's living with his grandson out on a ranch property near Masonville. I'd start there if you can. Let me see if I have the address. He usually sends a Christmas card."

She pulled out an address book and flipped through it. I was amazed at the neat little listings on each page with checkmarks for cards sent and received for the last few years.

Who is that organized?

I usually forget to send any cards and then feel bad and send a group email on the day after Christmas when I realize that I'm not going to get any cards out for the year. And that's in a good year. In a bad year, I don't do anything and then feel guilty. (But not guilty enough it seems to do better the next year.)

"Ah, yes. Here you go." She wrote out the address for me on a slip of paper and handed it across.

"Thank you. I appreciate that."

"You're welcome. And, here, let me send you with a couple slices of bread for him. Help you warm him up a bit." She winked at me. "He can be a little crotchety with people he doesn't know well."

I stared at the Tupperware container, wondering if the slices of bread would still be there by the time I reached his place or if I'd succumb to the temptation to eat them myself. (I wasn't proud of the thought, but pumpkin bread was a lot more tasty than Saltines and it really did help to keep snacking on something throughout the day.)

She caught my look and laughed. "And, here, another slice for you for the road. Do you want to leave Fancy with me while you go out there?"

"Is that okay? I mean, I know it's silly to worry about leaving her alone, she literally spends eighty percent of her day sleeping, but I also know that she's far more content when she can do that near someone."

"Of course. Dogs are social creatures, too. Plus, I like the company. I assume she can have a little bit of pumpkin bread?"

"Pumpkin is one of her favorites. Absolutely. Thank you so much, Lesley."

She walked me to the door and Fancy watched me leave with a look of absolute betrayal on her face, but I'm pretty sure she forgot who I was as soon as Lesley offered her that bite of pumpkin bread. At least I hoped so. There was a lot coming up in our lives that was going to require me to leave her behind more than either one of us was ready for.

CHAPTER 15

It was a nice day for a drive. Most of the aspens had already changed, but that's the beauty of evergreens, they stay ever green. And the Baker Valley has its own special beauty with the big mountains framing it in on all sides and the sprawling farmland. Not that anyone actually farms in the valley. Maybe hay. Lots of cattle, I think.

That's one of those things I don't pay much attention to. (Just like the fact that evergreens are not actually a specific type of tree even though that's what I'd always called them my whole life until I walked through an arboretum and realized that what I think of as evergreens are actually pine and spruce trees…Oops.)

It's funny the things you don't give much thought to if they don't directly impact you. And I'm the type to only keep the information I need in my brain and let everything else wash its way back out. (This would be why I have the lyrics to probably a thousand songs memorized but miss on details like that. Priorities. And really even there I'm not sure I know all the lyrics, more the shape of the song.)

Anyway.

The Ripley farm was down two dirt roads, tucked against the base of a mountain. There was a rusted blue pickup truck parked out front right next to a shiny new Ford F-250. It's easy to think about folks in rural areas being poor, and then you park your cheap as van next to their eighty-thousand-dollar vehicle and it puts things in perspective.

That was not a typo, by the way, with cheap as. I spent a little too much time around some New Zealanders back in the day. Learned to say sweet as and cool as and cheap as. At least I think it was the New Zealanders who said it. Could've been the Americans who brought it back when it turns out only five New Zealanders ever spoke like that. Language is funny that way.

I set aside my deep thoughts and parked my beat-up van that was probably going to require an actual back seat before the baby was born next to the shiny new truck and got out. Luckily, before I had to decide if I should look in the house or out in the barn or out in the field, a middle-aged woman came bustling my way from the barn. She had her hair pulled back in a long braid and was wearing jeans, a long-sleeved shirt, and work gloves.

"Can I help you?" she asked, all brisk efficiency.

"Looking for Adam Ripley? My…" What was Lesley? My step-grandfather's wife? That was a mouthful. "Uh, Lesley Pope told me I could find him here."

"Yeah, he's inside. What do you want with him?" She took off the gloves and tucked them into her back pocket.

"To talk about an old case he worked on."

She eyed me up and down. "You a cop?"

"Nope. But married to one. And he got the Chief's permission to let me see the file I was interested in."

She crossed her arms. "And what file was that?"

I wanted to say it was none of her business, but I figured that wasn't going to get me inside where it was actually warm. "Mary Diever. Old case. Thirty-six years ago. But they just ran some DNA on it, so it's back in the spotlight."

"And your involvement?"

I raised my eyebrows. "There any chance we can have this interrogation inside where it's warm? And where I won't have to repeat myself because I'm sure Mr. Ripley will have the same questions."

"Oh, you won't have to repeat yourself. Come on."

She led me through the front door, depositing her work gloves and boots just inside. When I went to take off my boots, too, she waved me off. "Unless you've been mucking stalls?"

"No, can't say I have."

"Then you're fine."

She led the way down a narrow hall to a large kitchen. "Hey, Pop. Visitor for you. Says she's looking into the Mary Diever murder and has the Chief's permission to look at the file. Wanted to ask you some questions."

A large, bald man looked up from the table, setting aside his newspaper as he assessed me. "Heard you'd been poking your nose into this case."

"Have we met?"

He leaned back, crossing his arms and giving me the once over. "No. But Maggie May Carver has a certain reputation amongst my fellow officers. None of us take kindly to civilians thinking they can do a better job than we can."

Even if I had?

"The Chief said it was okay for me to look into this one."

He snorted and took a sip of his coffee.

As the silence started to stretch into something awkward, I figured I'd try small talk. "So, how long have you been retired for?"

"Twenty years."

"Any chance you know my grandpa, Lou Carver?"

"Yep."

Well, this was fun. About like pulling teeth out.

"Um, oh, I almost forgot. This is for you." I handed across Lesley's pumpkin bread. "Lesley thought you'd like it."

He opened the container and smelled the bread suspiciously, but then smiled and nodded. "Pumpkin. One of my favorites. Tell her thank you for me."

"I will. Can I...sit?"

He shrugged as he broke off a small piece of the bread and munched on it. I sat and watched in envy, but didn't say anything, hoping he'd maybe participate in the conversation I was trying to have with him. No dice.

"Um, so, yeah, the reason I came by was because there was no sign of a coroner's report in the file."

"Didn't have one." He took another bite of bread, not even bothering to look at me.

I sat back. "No one looked at the body?"

"Someone looked, but no report needed. We weren't paper-pushers back in the day."

It felt like there was a dig somewhere in that sentence but I couldn't figure out where. "Do you remember what the findings were?"

He closed the Tupperware container and shoved it aside, finally looking at me once more. "Likely hit in the head with a rock. No signs of other violence. Had sex shortly beforehand."

I nodded. "We did see that part in your notes. Nothing else?"

He leaned back and crossed his arms, glaring at me. "What do you think you know?"

Until that moment, nothing, but the way he'd reacted made it pretty clear there'd been something else found during the examination. But what? Drugs? Would they have tested for that? Mary Diever being such a good girl and all? Not likely.

So what then?

I tilted my head to the side. Maybe…

Should I take that gamble? If I was wrong it was going to be ugly. But then again, this was already the most awkward and uncomfortable interview I'd ever conducted. "I was wondering if whoever looked at the body discovered her pregnancy," I said, trying not to show that it was just a guess.

He leaned forward, planting his elbows on the table. "Mary Diever was a good girl."

"So I've been told."

"What makes you think she'd been pregnant?"

Been pregnant, not *was* pregnant. Interesting. If he hadn't just misspoken that was.

I tried to keep it casual, just tilting my head slightly. "A little word here or there. Nothing specific. Why didn't you note it in the file?"

He sat back, crossing his arms once more. "Like I said, Mary Diever was a good girl. No need to ruin her name over something that wasn't relevant to the investigation."

"Even if the father could've been the killer?" I asked.

"He wasn't."

"How do you know?"

He glared me down. "Because it happened months before and the father didn't know about it."

"How do you know that?"

"Her father told me." He reopened the Tupperware container and started in on the last slice of bread, clearly agitated.

"What exactly did he tell you?"

"That Mary got in the family way with a boy she met from out of town. The boy never knew. He was gone before Mary even knew she was pregnant."

"What happened to the baby?"

He finished the bread and shoved the container back at me. "Adoption. Out of state. Her mother's cousin. Philadelphia I think it was. Father didn't know until it was all over."

I thought it through. "Was this the year she was supposed to be in college?"

He nodded.

"Did you confirm it with anyone? Other than her father, that is."

"I didn't need to. Roger Diever was a well-respected member of this community. I trusted his word."

"And the reason it wasn't in the file?"

"The fact that Mary Diever gave birth to a child out of wedlock had nothing to do with her murder almost six months later. That was over."

"Are you sure of that?"

"Positive." He planted his hands on the table and glared at me. Speaking slowly and clearly, he said, "Evan Browers was seen leaving the woods shortly before Mary Diever's body was discovered. His shirt was found near her body. He killed her."

I leaned back, studying him carefully. "But you didn't arrest him. Why not?"

"We had no murder weapon."

"And? Was that it? Just the lack of a murder weapon?"

He lifted his chin. "It was an election year. The DA at the time didn't want to risk such a high profile loss. He refused to take the case until we had more evidence."

"And her dad was okay with that?"

"Of course not. Why do you think he drank himself to death? But he was a lawyer. He knew there was room for doubt in what we had."

I nodded, thinking. "Okay. Thank you for your time."

I stood to leave, but his words stopped me. "Evan Browers killed that girl."

I nodded again. No point in arguing with him. "If he did then maybe we can find the evidence to prove it this time around. Give Mary the closure she deserves."

I grabbed Lesley's Tupperware container and left.

As I pushed my way back out the front door, my gut was jumping, but I couldn't tell whether it was excitement because I finally had what felt like a good development in the case, or because I desperately needed to eat something to settle my stomach back down.

Either way, I had a mother's cousin in Philadelphia to find. But first, time to circle back to Evan.

CHAPTER 16

Evan Browers picked up on the first ring. "What have you found out? Do you know who killed her?"

"Hold your horses there. I just got started. You're lucky I've found anything out."

As I navigated my way back to the main highway, I gave a small nod of thanks to wireless ear buds that let me safely talk in the car. I love Fancy, but she's not very accommodating when I need to be on the phone.

"But you do know something," Evan said, undeterred.

"Perhaps."

"What is it? What did you find?"

I took a moment to collect my thoughts as I turned back onto the two-lane highway that led to Creek. Was there a delicate way to ask this? Not really. "Evan, did you know that Mary had a kid?"

"No. Are you sure?"

"Pretty sure. The original investigator on the case just told me about it. Said she gave birth about six months before she was killed. Turns out she didn't go away to college; she went away because she was pregnant. So you didn't know?"

"I had no idea…But that explains a few things."

"Like what?" I glared at the slow-moving truck in front of me, resigned to going under the speed limit for the rest of the drive because it just wasn't worth it to try to pass him.

"Well, we weren't together all that long. Just six weeks or so. But Mary kept bringing up getting married and having kids. I liked her. I mean, she was Mary Diever, I couldn't hope for anyone better than her. But it seemed very rushed. Especially the part about kids."

(I knew exactly how that felt.)

"Huh. Interesting. But you thought she was talking about future kids that the two of you would have, not one she'd already had?"

I finally gave up and passed the truck, remembering to smile and wave as I went by in case it was someone I knew. Living in the valley, the odds were pretty high, so I couldn't be as rude as I wanted to be to someone who clearly thought speed limits were not in fact a target but instead something to avoid at all costs.

"At the time I definitely thought it was about kids we'd have in the future. But given what you just told me…There was one time that she asked if I thought I could love a kid that wasn't mine. I assumed she meant adoption, but now…"

"Now you think it might've been about this kid she'd had? Raising it."

"Him."

"What?"

"She always talked as if we'd have a boy."

That was interesting. I wished I wasn't driving so I could be sure to make a note of it, but it wasn't something I was likely to forget. "So somewhere out there was a boy child that Mary Diever gave birth to and maybe wanted to get back."

"Maybe. If what that detective told you was true."

"Oh, I'm pretty sure it was. And you know what that sounds like to me?" I smiled even as I pulled up behind yet another too-slow vehicle.

"What?"

"A motive for murder. Did she ever mention a prior relationship to you? One that would've been the summer before she met you?"

"No. Nothing."

Fortunately this time the too-slow vehicle turned before I had to pass them. I waved as I gunned it past. Almost home. If I was lucky the road would be clear the rest of the way.

"The detective said it was some random stranger passing through town," I said. "Does that sound like Mary to you?"

"Not at all."

"Even though you said she kissed you right when you met?"

"She did kiss me pretty fast, but she was shy about the rest of it." He cleared his throat, clearly embarrassed. "It took about a month for that to happen."

"Interesting. So did she lie to her dad or did her dad lie to the cops?"

"I'd bet she lied to her dad. She was definitely scared of him. I'm actually surprised she told him about the pregnancy at all."

I pulled into the driveway and turned off the car. "Hm. Me, too. I wonder why she did that? Then again, can't exactly hide a baby if you decide to raise it." I pursed my lips, trying to think of next steps. "Well, sounds like I need to see if I can track down this cousin she supposedly stayed with. She mention anything about that?"

"Nope. No family other than her dad and grandpa that I knew of. She hardly even talked about her mom, though."

"What did she tell you about the year she was away?"

"She didn't. She mostly wanted to talk about me and my life or about our future. When I tried to bring up her past, her friends, any of that, she shut it down. I didn't think anything of it at the time, because she did it with a laugh and a smile, but looking back now, I clearly didn't know her that well, did I?"

"Ah, well. New relationships can be like that. Sometimes it's just nice to be with someone who doesn't know all that baggage, you know?"

He chuckled. "Yeah. I can see that."

"Okay, well thanks for the help. At least we have something to go on now. I'll let you know what I find out."

"Please, call any time. And thank you."

He hung up and I went into the house, ready to find what I could find on Mary Diever and her family.

CHAPTER 17

You'd think that everyone is online these days. And that tracking down someone's family is as simple as finding the right family tree on Ancestry. Sadly, that was not the case with Mary Diever. At all.

Three hours later, I had nothing. I hadn't even been able to prove that Mary's mother was from Philadelphia. Or find a wedding certificate for her parents.

I had nothing. Zilch. Nada. Squat.

So when Jamie showed up and informed me that she'd made me an appointment with her doctor and we had to leave immediately to make the appointment in time, I figured, why not? Time to put the nail in the coffin, so to speak.

(Yes, yes, having a child is a wonderful, glorious experience that no one should ever question or doubt. And if they do they must be a horrible aberration that probably shouldn't reproduce. Might I remind you that I am the same person who found a dead body and wanted to just leave it there rather than go through the hassle of getting involved? So, yeah, I am possibly one of those aberrations. Hate to break it to ya.)

The doctor's office was not located in the one medical center in the valley, but was instead in a converted single-story home at the edge of Masonville that was painted bright yellow with white trim. It even had a yard surrounded by a white picket fence. Talk about cheerful and happy.

It felt a little forced, to be honest. Like some intro to a horror movie or something. Happy splat horror. Or maybe it was just my state of mind coloring things a little dark.

"You will love Dr. Dillon," Jamie said as we walked up the two steps to reach the front door. "She is the best. She's about our age, actually. And just so nice. And understanding. And competent. I love her."

I almost turned around and walked back out. One, because cheerfulness overload. But, two, because sitting in the waiting room were Abe and Evan. I adore them, they are a wonderful couple and some of my favorite people in the valley. But that meant the inevitable, "what brings you here?" conversation and I was not ready for people to know just yet.

Unfortunately, they spotted me before I could run, so I made the best of it. "Abe. Evan. What brings you here?"

They grinned at each other. "It's our first ultrasound today," Abe said.

I must've looked puzzled, because they didn't wait for me to ask my stupid question before Evan gestured to the tall woman sitting next to him. "This is Amy. She's our surrogate."

"Ah, that makes more sense. I mean, modern day, gender, had me going for a second there, but yeah, a surrogate makes a lot more sense. Hi, nice to meet you.

So. You're a surrogate?"

She nodded, smiling with deep contentment. "Yes. I've had three kids of my own and now I try to help other couples find their joy. This will be my third surrogate pregnancy."

I blinked hard. "This is the *sixth* time you've been pregnant?"

"Yes. It's such a wonderful experience. To carry a life." She ran her hands along her belly which was just slightly visible.

"But the swollen feet and ligaments stretching and hemorrhoids and morning sickness and…"

"Oh, but it's worth it. To feel that life growing inside you. And to know that you were part of the creation of a living, breathing being. The fact that I can give a couple like Evan and Abe this gift. It's…special." She was so serene about it.

I just nodded and smiled. It was better than every spoken response that came to mind. I'd once had someone describe the passing of their grandmother in terms like that right after I lost my parents.

How it was so special and magical to be there by her side for those final moments. Whereas my personal experiences of death had been more like, "I'd really like to never repeat this experience again, thank you very much."

Fortunately, I had grown enough since then to acknowledge that we do not all experience the world the same way, so there was no point in my stomping on this woman's joy just because I thought she was crazy for going through childbirth *six times.*

I forced myself to smile at Evan and Abe. "That's fantastic you guys. I'm so happy for you. When are you due?"

"We'll figure that out today, but in about eight months. So, June or July?"

They were so happy I couldn't help but be happy for them. And July seemed so far away. That was manageable. It was more than midway through another year entirely. I could get on board with a July due date.

"What brings you here?" Abe asked with a sly grin.

(I had a feeling that whole, ooh you're pregnant look was going to get *real old* before I finally delivered.)

I waved in Jamie's direction. "Oh. I'm here because Jamie's thinking of doing a home birth and wanted to use my living room for it. So I thought I'd chat with her doctor and see if we could inject a bit of sanity into her thinking."

Jamie laughed and came back over to join us. "I do want to do a home birth. The idea of giving birth in some sterile medical environment just doesn't work for me."

From there the conversation devolved in ways I tried not to pay attention to. I settled instead for pacing what once was someone's living room, looking at all of the framed pictures on the walls of happy smiling babies dressed as flowers.

In the corner was one of those thumb boards, covered with photos of smiling moms with newborns in their arms. Hard to believe how many people did this thing every single day.

Jamie came over to join me when the conversation wound down, smiling at the photos with a peaceful anticipation that frightened me. I waved to Evan and Abe as they and their surrogate were led down the hallway for their appointment.

"By the way," Jamie said, "I told the receptionist to call for me not you, so don't worry that they'll find out before you're ready to tell them. Although, you are going to have to tell everyone at some point. Being pregnant isn't something you can hide."

"Wanta bet?"

"Maggie."

"What. Mary Diever hid her pregnancy. Although I'm not sure for how long. Seems she went away to have the kid so maybe she was gone before she started to show."

"Really?"

I nodded. "Yep. According to the original investigator. Gave birth about six months before she was killed. Supposedly she went to Philadelphia to stay with some cousin of her mother's, but I can't find any sign of the mom before she arrived here, let alone the cousin."

"Interesting."

I nodded, but before we could talk about it further, Abe and Evan were back with photos from their ultrasound. I honestly couldn't tell what I was looking at except it was black and white, but they seemed very excited.

Fortunately for us the receptionist waited until they'd left before she looked at me with a knowing smile. "Ready to see the doctor?"

Since "no" wasn't an acceptable answer, I nodded and followed her, Jamie at my side. Truth time.

CHAPTER 18

The receptionist led us down the hallway and to a room on the left. There was a room on the right, too, but that door was closed. As we waited for the doctor to join us, I looked around the examining room.

It's weird to have a doctor's visit in what once was someone's bedroom. It wasn't unprofessional in the least, but there was just this strange disconnect in not having the sterility I was used to in a standard doctor's visit. I think it was the colors. They were warm instead of cool because she'd left in the brown wood paneling on the walls. I'm used to white walls, you know. Bright, glaring, white walls. Clean walls.

(Not that these were dirty, but they could've been and I'd never have known it. I like that in my own home, hides the dust, but not in the doctor's office.)

At least the floor wasn't carpet. That would've been a step too far for my secretly germophobic soul. I may not like to clean, but I very much do not like smells and I can imagine in a doctor's office things would accumulate in carpet. (And now that we've had that unpleasant thought together...)

There was a light knock at the door and a woman with dark hair streaked the slightest bit gray stepped into the room, smiling. "Hi. I'm Dr. Dillon. You must be Maggie." She held a hand out to me and I took it. She had a firm grip, but soft hands. "Jamie's told me a bit about you."

"Why, because she's known I was pregnant this whole time even though I didn't?"

She laughed as she washed her hands in the sink. Her laugh was warm like the room. "No. I was curious about the barkery and café and the plans for the pet resort. I love to cook, but the thought of turning that love into a business is a daunting one. Not that I would, mind you. I didn't attend all those years of medical school to become a baker. Although, there are days when that seems very appealing."

"Oh, that makes sense."

She smiled at Jamie. "But she did make me promise to fit you in as soon as possible if you ever asked."

I rubbed at the back of my neck. "I didn't realize I was pregnant, you know. I just figured I was stress-eating."

"It happens."

"I haven't been taking folic acid. And I drink Coke. A lot."

She squeezed my shoulder. "There's actually not as much caffeine in a Coke as there is in a cup of coffee. Which means you're probably better off than a coffee-drinker who doesn't know they're pregnant." She smiled at me. "Let's make a deal. We won't worry about the baby's health until there's something to worry about. Your body and mind are going to have enough to deal with in the next little bit without adding in additional concerns."

Clearly this woman did not know me well, but I just nodded.

"Now. First things first, let's get you to pee in a cup so we can confirm this pregnancy, and then we'll see what we can see with an ultrasound."

"Okay."

Jamie laughed. "You're going to be fine, Maggie. Trust us. It's…it's great."

"For you, maybe. You wanted all of this. I wanted to live a life that involved curling up on my couch with a good book and a dog at my feet."

"And you will have that. You'll just also have a gorgeous man who adores you and adorable little kids that have his eyes and your spirit."

I flinched. "Can we flip that around? Let them have his calm demeanor and my eyes instead?"

Her laughter followed me down the hallway.

🐾 🐾 🐾

Five minutes later it was official. I was in fact pregnant.

"Congratulations," Dr. Dillon said. "Now let's see what there is to see."

She had me lie down on the table and lift up my shirt and unbutton my jeans so she could get to my belly.

"We'll start with this type of ultrasound. But if you're not that far along then we'll move to the other option."

Since I really didn't want to know what the other option was, I just nodded my head and closed my eyes.

"Don't close your eyes. You'll want to see this. Trust me."

She dimmed the lights. It was all oddly peaceful and soothing. The gel she used on my belly was warm and smelled like baby powder. She ran the little transducer firmly along my belly, her eyes focused on the black and white monitor we could all see.

"Ha. Look. Right there."

I stared at the screen. There were two large dark spaces, each filled with a white blob. Kid-shaped blobs.

Tears filled my eyes. Not because I was sad. But just because it's an overwhelming moment to see that you're carrying two living, breathing beings inside of you. (Don't worry. I cried plenty later over the idea of twins, trust me. But in that moment it was awe overwhelm not freaking out panic.)

"Twins," I managed to say.

"Yes."

I glanced at Jamie who was crying in happiness.

"Don't. You're going to make me cry, too." And then it hit me. "Oh no. Matt should be here for this. Oh no. I've messed up, haven't I? He was supposed to be here. And I can't fake it if we do it again. You only get that overwhelmed feeling once."

I'd been so concerned with whether I really was pregnant I hadn't even thought that this was one of those big moments you share with your spouse. And now it was too late. I could try to schedule another appointment and lie to him, but then I'd be lying to him. And he was my husband. I didn't want to lie to him, not about something as important as this.

I really did cry then.

"Don't worry, Maggie. Matt will forgive you. Here. Call him. Right now. You can FaceTime."

So I did. Lying there in the doctor's office with our little twin terrors on the screen, I made a video call to my husband.

"Maggie? Is everything okay? You never call me at work." He was standing on the side of the road somewhere, the wind audible through our connection.

"It's fine. I just…Um, Jamie was able to get me a last-minute appointment at the doctor and I went with her without thinking about it."

"You're there now?"

I nodded.

"And?"

"And we're pregnant. Twins. Do you want to see? Jamie can hold the phone and it'll be just like you're here," I said, hopefully. Matt had been so great up until that moment that I really shouldn't have been nervous about his reaction, but I kept waiting for that one thing that he'd get really mad about.

"Of course. Give me a minute." He set the phone down and I heard some grunting and muttering and then a slamming door.

"What were you doing?" I asked when he picked the phone back up.

"Oh, arresting someone. But he's in the back of the squad car now. Let me see that ultrasound."

Jamie took the phone from me so he could see everything at once.

"Twins!" He laughed and did a little jig (at least that's what I think he did from the movement of the image on the screen). "Do we know the sex yet?"

Dr. Dillon answered, "If I had to guess, I'd say girls. But it's a little early yet."

"How far along do you think I am?" I asked.

There was a part of me that wanted to be a week from delivery just so I didn't have to think about it all. But the other part of me wanted something like five years to prepare.

"I'd say you're right around the fourteen week mark."

"So, forty weeks, minus fourteen, I have about twenty-six weeks to go? So like six months?"

She shook her head. "Actually, most twins deliver early. Generally around thirty-six weeks. Which means you have more like five months."

Matt cheered. "That's the best first-year anniversary present I could imagine. Twin baby girls."

I sighed. "And here I was hoping for a luxurious weekend at a resort where we never got out of bed all weekend and drank champagne and ate steak and chocolate until we were ready to burst."

"We'll do that for our ten-year anniversary. Or maybe our twentieth, depending on the kids and who we can get to watch them."

"Or twenty-fifth or thirtieth if you convince me to go through this more than once."

We smiled at each other, both thinking about spending that many years together.

Matt glanced away. "I better go. Guy I just arrested isn't exactly happy about me leaving him sitting in there."

"Love you."

"Love you, too. And love those little bumps."

Jamie hung up the phone for me.

"Well, what now?" I asked.

"Now we keep a good eye on things," Dr. Dillon replied. "You're what we used to call a geriatric pregnancy, which comes with some additional risks for both the babies and you. We'll want to test for birth defects, which fortunately we can do with a blood test for now. We can follow that up with amniocentesis if we have to later, but the blood test is always where I prefer to start. Less invasive."

"Geriatric pregnancy? I'm only thirty-seven." I sat up and tugged my shirt back into place.

"Any woman over thirty-five is considered a woman of advanced maternal age."

"Seriously?"

She smiled at me as she put away her equipment. "It's not a judgement. It's just the body. These things work a lot easier when you're younger."

I shook my head. "Lovely. Just lovely. Although I will point out that my body seemed to do an absolutely swell job of conceiving despite my advanced maternal age."

She laughed. "It happens that way sometimes. The ones who desperately want to get pregnant struggle and then someone who wasn't planning for it at all gets pregnant after one night. But it doesn't change the fact that being older and pregnant comes with some added risks."

"Yeah, fine, whatever."

We wrapped up the visit with a blood draw (not my favorite, but better than a giant needle going into my belly) and then Jamie and I headed home, her chatting the whole way about all the *things* I was going to need for the babies.

At some point I tuned her out for my own mental health. There was so much involved in bringing a kid into the world, let alone two at once, I just couldn't handle it yet.

All I wanted was to solve a murder and take a nap. And maybe eat a big greasy plate of French fries smothered in red chili and cheddar cheese. With a little extra hot sauce thrown on top for an added kick of flavor.

CHAPTER 19

The next day I'd just returned home from showing my grandpa and Lesley the ultrasound when Jamie called. "You free this afternoon?" she asked.

"Of course, I am. I have no life, Jamie."

"Maggie, your definition of no life and everyone else's are worlds apart. But be ready for me to pick you up at one."

"Why? What's up?" I pinned the ultrasound image to the fridge with an "I Love My Newfie" fridge magnet. If I was going to be one of those parents with the cluttered fridge, might as well start early.

"Mason's grandmother has requested our presence."

I shuddered. "Why?"

"Well, yours actually, but I'm to deliver you."

I shook my head even though she couldn't see it. "That woman scares me, Jamie. Why would I agree to meet her?"

"She said she has information related to your investigation."

"Really? How'd that come up?"

Jamie cleared her throat. "Mason and I had dinner with her at the club last night, and I may have mentioned what you told me about Mary Diever being pregnant and going away to give birth. I wondered out loud who the father was. At which point Mason's grandmother shot me a look of pure venom and told me that idle gossip was the Devil's work and to shut my trap about things I didn't know about."

"Ouch. That woman is not subtle."

"No, she is not. But then after dinner she pulled me aside and told me to bring you by today. So maybe she knows."

"Do I have to go? She scares me. Couldn't you just go and find out what she knows and then tell me about it?"

"No. She definitely wanted you. Plus, I kind of like her. She has spunk. Even when she's telling me I'm doing the Devil's work. So, one o'clock?"

I sighed. "Fine."

I had an hour to get ready. But what do you wear to go visit the matriarch of the valley? Do you try to dress up to her standards? To pretend that you can fit into her upper-class domain?

Or do you do what I did which is throw on a comfortable pair of jeans and a t-shirt that says Book Nerd on it in big bold letters because there's simply no point in trying to pretend that you belong somewhere you really don't?

My lack of dress-up meant I had plenty of time left to call Evan before I left. I figured maybe he'd know why Mason's grandmother had information on Mary Diever.

But the phone went to voicemail. Odd, considering how fast he'd picked up the last time I'd called, but I shrugged it off. People can't always answer the phone immediately.

Still. I flagged it for follow-up later. Now was not the time for Evan to decide to go on the run or something equally foolish.

🐾 🐾 🐾

Jamie glanced at my outfit when she came to pick me up, but she didn't say anything about it. She was in an adorable purple dress that accented her baby bump. She also had full make-up on and her hair was curled and styled, something that had probably taken twenty minutes to get looking so carelessly cute.

To be fair to me, I had at least thrown on some mascara and lip gloss. But any make-up routine that would require more than a minute of effort was beyond me and had been even when I was in a corporate job.

We chatted about more baby stuff as we drove to the house which was set halfway up a mountainside outside of Masonville, only reached along a long, winding road through the trees.

I don't know why, but the whole time we were driving up that road I kept thinking about Medieval times and how you'd enter a castle that had murder holes where if the person didn't like you they could shoot you or drop something on your head.

"She's actually pretty nice, you know," Jamie said as we pulled up outside a large but not overly ostentatious home.

"Jamie, you'd say a wounded pit viper was pretty nice as it tried to strike you."

"Don't be silly. Come on. She doesn't bite at least."

"Well, that's one plus," I muttered as I reluctantly followed her to the front door.

A woman in a maid's uniform met us at the door and led us into what could only be described as a parlor.

There were floral couches surrounded by small tables, each with one incredibly delicate and breakable item on it.

Mason's grandmother was seated on one of the couches, her wheelchair discretely placed behind it.

"I'd rise to greet you, but these legs are not cooperating today."

I hadn't realized that some wheelchair users can actually walk on a limited basis until I had a co-worker who was in a wheelchair my first job out of college. It seemed Mason's grandmother was like that as well.

"It's good to see you Grammie," Jamie said, bending down to give her a kiss on the cheek.

Mason's grandmother caught my surprised expression and cackled. "I let her call me that because she's nice. And she's family. *You* call me Mrs. Mason. My husband's been dead twenty years, but I earned it."

"Of course, Mrs. Mason. Thank you for seeing us."

I wondered if I was expected to step forward and kiss her hand or something, but she waved towards the couch. "Sit. Jamie tells me you're poking into the Mary Diever murder."

I nodded. "Evan Browers asked me to. He said he's innocent, but he thinks they're going to charge him because he was involved with her and they were together that morning."

"Fool boy. Getting mixed up with that girl."

"Everyone says she was a good girl," I responded, curious how she'd react.

She harrumphed. "Any women say that or was it just men who didn't know her well?"

"Men."

"Figures. A woman bats her big eyes at a man and

suddenly she's the best of all girls. I'm sure you've seen that one yourself."

Pit viper, I tell you. I cleared my throat and decided to come back swinging. "The original investigator said she might have left town to give birth to a child the year before she was killed. Maybe stayed with a cousin of her mother's, but I can't find any record of her mother or this supposed cousin. You know anything about that?"

She cackled again. "You have moxie. I like that."

"Thank you. But you didn't answer the question."

The maid came in to serve us tea just then and we sat in silence until she'd left again. Mrs. Mason studied me as she sipped her tea, her pinky finger raised slightly. "Mary's mother, Genevieve, wasn't what she seemed. The Dievers would have us believe that she was part of society. A real blue blood. A debutante. But I had family who were part of society in Philadelphia and they'd never heard of her."

"Just because *your* relatives hadn't…"

"My relatives knew every family worth knowing," she snapped. "If Genevieve Diever grew up in Philadelphia and they didn't know her, then she wasn't someone worth knowing." She took another sip of her tea, studying me, clearly waiting for my comeback.

There were so many things wrong with what she'd said that I didn't know how to respond. Finally I said, "I've heard that gossip is the Devil's work."

"Ha. So it is. But what I know is not gossip. I hired a private investigator."

I choked on my tea. "Really? Why?"

Back then that had to have been pretty expensive.

She raised her chin. "Because a woman I didn't know

showed up in my territory and tried to put on airs that she was too good to associate with me. I didn't like that. I wanted to know who she was that she thought so much of herself."

I narrowed my eyes. "Did she actually try to put on airs? Or did her husband and father-in-law try to do so on her behalf?"

"Ah, very good. It was her father-in-law. But I couldn't let the insult stand, so I looked into it." She sipped at her tea again, a small smile on her face.

"And what did you find?"

"That Genevieve Diever had been a dancer at a men's club in Atlantic City. Not a drop of society blood in her veins. Not only that, but she married Roger Diever when she was already six months pregnant."

"I don't understand. Why did Roger Diever marry her then? From what Mason said, he was a social climber. He could've just walked away from her and the kid. And nothing I've heard said he was such a loving father that the existence of a baby would've changed his mind."

She nodded. "I don't know for sure, but I suspect it was because it put him in control. That man was cold and mean and any woman who could would've avoided marrying him. But a woman in a bad circumstance? Who saw him as some sort of savior? And saw Colorado as a chance to wipe the slate clean? She'd take that chance. And because he knew her secret he'd always have the power. She could never leave him. Not without losing everything."

I set down my tea and grabbed my notepad to jot down a few notes. "It seems plausible, but how can you be sure that's what happened?"

She smiled and I wondered exactly who was calling whom cold. "I'm positive about *her* motivations and how he used her past against her, because after my investigator returned with his information, I confronted her with it. Over tea. Right here in this living room."

"What did she do?"

"Cried. Confessed it all to me. Told me about how he hurt her. About how she wanted out, but didn't know how to leave and not lose her daughter."

I stared up at her, suddenly cold. "When was this?"

She took another sip of her tea before answering me. "About a month before she died."

"And you didn't tell anyone? What if he killed her? What if her death wasn't from natural causes?"

She set the cup aside. "Oh, I'm quite certain he did kill her."

"But…Why not tell anyone?"

"Because I had something much bigger to protect." She folded her hands in her lap and sat up with perfect posture. "Since I was a young woman I have been a part of a network that stretches across the entire country that helps abused women flee their abusers. When they're ready to run we pass them along, find them new identities, new jobs, and new lives. We make it so their abusers can never again touch them. If they have kids, we include the kids."

"But then…"

She took a deep breath and stared me down. "We can't jeopardize what we do for one woman. Which is why when we lose one before she can escape, we have to let it go."

"But that left Mary…"

She nodded. "Alone with her mother's abuser. Yes."

I swallowed heavily. "Did he…?"

"Hurt her? Not that I'm aware of. I would have done something if I thought he had. No. He spent a lot of time in Denver and he kept a woman there who I am certain he did hurt. Even so. When Mary was old enough that I thought she'd keep the secret, I told her about her mother, and I told her that if she ever was in need of my help to let me know."

"Which is why she came to you when she got pregnant."

"Yes. I don't know who the father was before you ask. All I know is that she was scared, very scared that he would find out. She came to me and asked me to help her. Told me she couldn't have anyone know about the pregnancy. Asked if I could send her somewhere until it was time to deliver."

She pressed her lips together. "I told her it would be easier if she didn't have the child at all, but she insisted. I think she loved the man, whoever he was. So we arranged for it to look like she was going away to university, but she actually went to stay with someone I knew until the baby was born. She came home a couple months after that when the school year would have ended. No one but the two of us knew."

"Her father did. He told the investigator about it"

She shook her head. "Not beforehand, he didn't. He believed she'd received a scholarship and was attending classes. The woman she stayed with was in the same city as the university she was supposed to be attending. And she was accepted at that university. She planned to return and attend the next year. If she could finish her degree in three years, no one would ever be the wiser."

"Which means her father found out at some point *after* she returned."

She shrugged. "Most likely. I wouldn't know. We didn't speak after I arranged for her to go away. It wouldn't have been safe to do so."

"Did she try to speak to you at any point after she returned?"

She nodded sharply. "She came by the house the week before she was murdered. But I had my maid send her away. Like I said, it wouldn't have been safe for us to speak."

I chewed on my lip, thinking. "You said she was scared of the baby's father finding out."

"Yes. Very."

"But you didn't know who he was. Could the woman she stayed with know?"

"It's possible. I have the contact information for her. She's still part of the network." She took out an address book and jotted down a name and phone number.

When I reached for the slip of paper, she didn't release it right away, instead staring at me intensely. "Some things are best left in the past. If it was this man who killed Mary and not Evan Browers, then he killed the woman who gave birth to his child. He won't take kindly to you resurrecting the dead."

I snatched the piece of paper away. "I realize that. But he also shouldn't be allowed to live his life without any consequence for what he did. If he killed her, he should pay for that."

She raised one eyebrow, but didn't say more about it.

The conversation then turned to Jamie's pregnancy and her plans for the nursery. At least she'd finally found the right shade of yellow. But as they chatted about that, my mind was focused on who the mysterious father could be and where Mary Diever's child was now.

CHAPTER 20

The first thing I did when I returned home was call the number Mrs. Mason had given me.

"Margie Price," the woman on the other end of the line said, her voice thick with, of all things for someone living in Philadelphia, a southern accent.

"Ms. Price. I was given your number by a Mrs. Mason in Colorado. She sent a young lady to live with you about thirty-six years ago, Mary Diever."

"Was that her last name? I never knew. We try to keep these situations as protected as possible. I only knew her as Mary Smith."

I settled onto the couch and put my feet up. "So you remember her?"

"I do. Sweet young lady, but scared of her own shadow. I suspect the men in her life had not been kind."

I reached for my notepad. "She talked to you about that?"

"Mm. Well, not exactly, but one can always tell these things. My now-husband would come by every few days and Mary always hid away when he did. Shied away from men at the grocery store as well. Kept to herself, poor thing."

Interesting. I tapped my pen against my lips, trying to think what to ask next. "I don't know if you're aware of this, but Mary Diever was killed the summer after she stayed with you."

"She was? Oh dear. That poor child. I really shouldn't call her a child, she was eighteen at the time. But there was always something very young and innocent about her."

I frowned, because that didn't seem in line with some of what Evan Browers had said. "Did you see any signs that she was a drinker or into drugs?"

"Oh, that."

"So you did?"

She huffed in annoyance. "That only started after the baby was born. She found it very hard to let go and needed an escape. Poor thing had to stay with me four months after the baby was born so her daddy wouldn't know why she'd come here. And there wasn't much else for her to do. So, yes, she did start drinking and doing some drugs. But nothing too bad. Just a kid trying to cover her pain."

"You said she found it very hard to let go? Did she want to keep the baby?"

"Not initially. The day of the birth there was no problem at all. She gave that little boy up as quick as you please. But then she had all that time to think. I know it weighed on her. She didn't say anything then, but you could see it in how she looked at other babies and how she cried sometimes."

"You said she didn't say anything then. Did she say something later?"

"Why yes she did. She called me about a month or two after she'd gone back home and asked me if I knew where the baby was and if there was any way she could change her mind and get it back."

I sat up straighter. "When exactly was this?"

"I don't know. July maybe? She'd been gone for a bit by then."

"Did she tell you why she wanted to try to get the baby back?"

"Um. Well. Not sure how smart it was, but she said she'd met a man who loved her very much and she thought he'd be a good father and might be willing to raise her child with her."

I scribbled that down as I asked, "And what did you tell her?"

"That it was too late. That she should marry that man if he loved her, but to let the baby go. Her only chance of reversing the adoption at that point was having the father come forward and challenge it. They'd just started allowing DNA paternity testing, but it wasn't very common yet, so even that wasn't a certainty."

I nodded to myself, thinking it through. "I bet that's when she told her father. He was a lawyer. Maybe she thought he could challenge the adoption for her. But he obviously didn't."

"Not that I know of. That call was the last I heard of it."

"Do you know where the baby is now?" I asked, just in case, because I suspected we were going to need to prove who the father was at some point and DNA was our best hope.

There was a long silence on the other end of the line and then she finally said, "It was a private adoption."

"Yes, but, do you know where the baby is now?"

Another long silence.

"Look, Ms. Price. Someone killed Mary Diever. And if it wasn't the man who was going to maybe marry her and help her raise that baby, then it was very likely the man who fathered the child. If we can get a DNA sample from the child, then we can maybe figure out who that was."

She sniffed. "Oh, I'm pretty sure I know who the father was."

"You do? How?" And how did she remember after all these years. It's nice to have the information you need fall into your lap and all, but color me skeptical that she'd remember the name of some random baby daddy thirty-six years after the fact.

"He came to visit while she was here. He was quite memorable."

"How did that happen? He wasn't supposed to know she was pregnant."

"Oh, he didn't. Not until that visit at least."

"What happened?" I asked, thinking about how horrible that must've been for Mary to have the man show up on her doorstep like that.

"Well, as you know, Mary was supposed to be here for school. That's what her daddy believed. Now, she told him she couldn't go back for the holidays because of the travel time and all. Truth being she was about to pop. That girl gave birth in January. But about a month before that, I'd say early December, her daddy called and told her that a friend was going to be in town and had a few Christmas presents for her that he was going to drop by."

"Couldn't she refuse? Or just be out when the man dropped by?"

"That's what she tried to do. Hid in her room as soon as he showed up here. But it didn't work."

"Why? What happened?"

"Well, the man came by, and I told him Mary wasn't here, but he insisted on staying until she returned. Sat in my living room for four hours. Finally, I suggested he just go on now because I really wasn't sure when she'd return, but he said he was prepared to stay there all weekend if he must."

"That's strange, isn't it?"

"It would be, if he weren't the father of the baby. At least, that's what I figured after his reaction when he finally did see her."

My stomach grumbled, but I didn't dare move to get something. I was too fascinated by her story. "So Mary finally gave up and came into the room?"

"Oh my, yes."

"And what happened then?"

"He grabbed her by the arm. Shook her. Got in her face and demanded to know what she was doing pregnant. Hissed under his breath, asking her why she hadn't gotten rid of it." She made a disgusted noise before she added, "And then that man had the audacity to suggest that she get rid of it right then even though a fool could see it was too late for that. Poor girl. She started sobbing, telling him she was sorry, begging his forgiveness. I honestly don't know what would've happened next because he was fixing to take her away from there."

"What did you do?"

"I told him I was fixing to call the cops and that he better get the hell out of there right then if he knew what was good for him."

"Did you?"

"Yes, ma'am. Soon as I started dialing, he took off. But when the cops arrived, Mary refused to speak about it. Wouldn't even give them his name." She tsked, still clearly annoyed after all these years.

"So how do you know who he is? If you just saw him that one day and then he ran off and Mary wouldn't name him."

She took a deep breath. "Oh, well, see, I've seen his face on TV. He's a senator. That mouthy one with too many opinions."

"He's a *senator*? Really?" I tried to think about who I knew from the Baker Valley who'd run for the Senate. There was only one.

"Well, at least he was. I believe he was just defeated in the latest election. Good riddance and God speed. Your voters finally got a bit of sense."

I covered my mouth with my hand for a moment, horrified by what this could mean if the father of Mary Diever's baby really was who Margie thought he was.

"Just to be clear, you're saying the man who hurt Mary and was likely the father of her child was Senator Quentin Baker."

"Yes. Although he obviously wasn't a senator back then."

"Oof."

Senator Quentin Baker was one of the most well-respected and well-known men in the valley, maybe even in the state. A man who lived and breathed family values. And had to be seventy-five now?

Seventy-five minus thirty-six was thirty-nine. Which meant that upstanding, very married father of three Quentin Baker had been involved with a seventeen-year-old and not in a nice, loving supportive relationship either.

But that might explain why everyone was so determined to sweep things under the rug back then. Because if he wasn't the DA at the time, then he was probably the judge. I wrote the name on my notepad and circled it three times.

Quentin Baker. Yikes.

"Did you ever see him again?" I asked. "Did he try to come back after the cops were gone?"

"No. I was worried about it for a bit there. Had my boyfriend stay over just in case and didn't let Mary go anywhere alone until after she'd delivered. But I never saw hide nor hair of him again. A few hang-up calls, so he may have tried to get through, but that was it. She told him before he left that she was giving the baby away, so maybe that was enough once he got cooled down some."

"And what about the baby? Are you sure he didn't go after the baby?"

"The baby was fine."

"How do you know?"

She paused.

"Ms. Price. Please. How do you know the baby was fine?"

"Because I was a nurse at the hospital where he was born. And that dark hair and those gray eyes were very distinctive. He also had a birth mark on his neck, one of those wine stain ones."

"So you know his name?"

"Yes."

"And do you know where to find him now? If we needed to get a DNA sample, could we?"

She didn't answer.

"Margie? It may be the only way we can prove who killed Mary Diever. Will you tell me how to find him if I need to?"

She sighed. "Yes. But only if you need to. He is a good man who does not need to find out that his mama was killed so soon after he was born."

It wasn't ideal, but it would have to do for now. "Thank you. I appreciate it."

"You're welcome. Just watch yourself. That Quentin Baker was one of the scariest men I've ever crossed paths with. Meet him on the street and he'd seem like the nicest man in the world, but he is not. I am telling you, steer clear of that man if you can."

"I'll keep that in mind. Thanks again."

I hung up the phone and stared at the wall.

Senator Quentin Baker. A man at the start of an illustrious career. A man with a lot to lose if Mary Diever came forward about having his baby…

Definitely a motive for murder in my book. Of course, I had a feeling no one was going to want me to pursue this one step further once I told them who the new suspect was. Which meant maybe I should just keep that to myself for a bit longer.

CHAPTER 21

I was trying to figure out how exactly to pursue this new lead without bringing the world down on my head when my phone rang. Caller ID said it was Matt, but he never calls me when he's at work, so I answered immediately.

"Matt, what is it? What's wrong?"

He hesitated for an extra second. "It's Evan Browers."

"What happened to him?"

"We don't know. They found his truck at the west end of the valley, abandoned. There was a note on the seat."

My stomach clenched. He better not have given up on me just when I was starting to make progress in his case. "What kind of note?"

Matt hesitated again. "It was a confession, Maggie."

"A confession to what?" I stood and started pacing the room.

"What do you think?"

"Mary Diever's murder? No. Why on earth would a man ask me to investigate the murder and then turn around and confess when I'm finally starting to make progress on the investigation?"

"Because you unearthed the secret that made him kill

her. According to the note, he killed Mary in a jealous rage because he found out she'd had another man's child."

I shook my head even though he couldn't see it. "That doesn't make sense. She had that child before they even met. And he didn't know about the baby until I told him, I'd swear to it. Plus he still loves her even now."

"People do strange things for love."

"No."

"I'm just telling you what the note said, Maggie."

"So it was a suicide note?"

"No. He's on the run."

I scoffed. "That makes even less sense. Who tells the authorities they're going on the run? If you decide to run you hide the fact as long as you possibly can so you can get a good head start."

"Thought about that a lot have you?"

I glared at the wall because I couldn't glare at Matt in person. "Don't be smart with me. You met Evan, did he strike you as that stupid? To confess to a murder and then tell everyone he was running away?" I shook my head. "No. It doesn't make any sense. It's a set-up. You have to find him, Matt. He's in danger if he isn't already dead."

He sighed. "Sometimes people do things that don't make sense."

I shook my head again. "If you won't look for him, I will. I'm going to his place. See if there are any signs of foul play."

"Maggie. This is not your job."

"No, it's yours. But if you aren't going to do it, then I am."

I could almost see him frowning at me through the phone. "Maggie, please. If you're right about Evan then going to his place could be dangerous."

"Then come pick me up so we can go together."

He didn't answer, so I added, "Fine. If you don't want to come with me then you can sit there and nervously wait for me to contact you and tell you everything's okay, not knowing if I'm alive or not for the next hour."

(I didn't get out of my high school curfew by playing nice.)

He sighed, a deep heavy sigh full of defeat. I crossed my arms and waited.

"Okay. I'll be there in a few minutes. Do not leave until I get there. But you have to understand that whether he wrote that note or not, it may be impossible to clear his name at this point."

"Why? It's just one piece of evidence."

"That the press were tipped off to. They found the truck first. Evan Browers' confession is going to run on the evening news tonight. Oh, and the DNA results came back today with a match to Evan. Those leaked as well."

I glanced at my notepad where the name Quentin Baker was circled.

"Matt, think about what you just told me and ask yourself if you really think there isn't someone behind those two leaks who's trying to frame Evan Browers. Someone who's very media-savvy and somehow knew I was getting too close."

"Maggie, no one thinks like that in the real world."

I laughed, once. "Politicians do. Like Quentin Baker, the likely father of Mary's baby."

"What?" he snapped.

"Yeah, that's the phone call I just had. The woman Mary stayed with was pretty sure Quentin Baker was the father. He showed up before she gave birth and was furious to find out she was pregnant."

"Maggie, you need to step back from this right now. Quentin Baker is not someone you want to mess with." He'd gone from casual to full alert.

"But if I don't, who will? I mean, look at poor Evan. Thirty-six years of being a murder suspect and then framed for it when someone actually gets close to the truth? I can't step back because no one else will step forward."

"Look, I'll tell the Chief. Let him figure out how to proceed. He won't go after Evan with what you've found."

"Come on now, Matt. You know that isn't true. Between that note, the abandoned vehicle, and the DNA match, do you honestly think Evan Browers is going to get a fair trial? Actually, do you honestly think he'll be alive to go to trial? Much cleaner to get rid of him. A nice little staged suicide and it's all wrapped up with a bow."

I shook my head. "No. We need to pursue this right now. If we wait for some bureaucrat to make a decision, it could mean Evan's life. So, are you going to pick me up so we can go over to his place together? Or am I doing this myself?"

He let out a deep, exasperated breath. "I'll be there in twenty. Wait for me."

"Okay. Love you."

"Love you, too," he muttered.

(It was the type of love you, too, that a man says when he really does love you but there's a part of him that really wishes you had an ounce of sense or had taken up macrame as a hobby instead of murder.)

CHAPTER 22

Evan Browers' house was actually nice. I don't know why that surprised me so much, probably because I can be as narrow-minded and biased as the next person, so I'd assumed that a man who was basically shunned by everyone and was big and scary looking would live in some run-down dump of a place with rotted out car parts littering the front lawn.

But it wasn't like that at all. There was enough snow on the ground I couldn't see the yard, but it was pretty clear he put a lot of effort into his home. It was freshly-painted a soft shade of blue with white trim and all of the windows and doors were well-maintained. It wasn't a big place, but it was nice.

Matt tried the door and it opened for him so we carefully walked inside, looking around for any signs of foul play. (I watch too many true crime shows, sorry.)

Everything seemed in order. There was a small table with two chairs in the kitchen that had a stack of business papers tucked against the wall. The fridge was full and was another surprise. Evan Browers hadn't struck me as the type to like organic yogurt and fresh vegetables, but that was what was in there.

(The large freezer in the garage full of hand-labeled portions of elk meat that we found later eased my mind a bit. At least I hadn't been completely off about the man.)

There were two bedrooms, one with a small bed tucked into the corner. That room had the cold, dusty feel of a room that wasn't used much. The other bedroom had a large bed, perhaps even custom built, that dominated the space.

The living room, hallway, and both bedrooms had wildlife photos hung on the walls, each framed in an identical simple black frame. The photos were really good. The type that make you feel like you could reach out and touch the animal in the photo.

"What does Evan Browers do for a living?" I asked Matt, studying an image of a bear about to eat a fish.

"Wildlife photography. He posts to stock photography sites mostly, but also sells prints off his website."

"So these are all his?"

I looked at the pictures more closely. Impressive. It's one thing to know that someone out there has that kind of skill, but another thing entirely to realize that the strange man you just met has that kind of skill.

"He's exceptionally good," I said.

"I know. I almost bought one of his prints. He has one that's of a deer in a meadow just as the sun's coming up. It's stunning. But I figured buying artwork from a man you're going to arrest for murder was poor form."

"I don't know about that. Could've helped the man eat for a few days in the meantime." I stared at the photos on the wall again. "You know, if we get through this and he's not arrested or killed for some fool reason, I'm going to ask him to do a series of photos of Fancy, Lulu, and Hans. I think it would be really neat to include their photos somehow at the new pet resort. I'm not sure how yet. I'll know once I see the photos. If he's willing that is."

"I like that idea. Maybe you should have a local artists gallery, too. Let visitors buy artwork while they're there."

"Ooh, I like that. We could have Evan's photography and I know Melinda Nederland does some gorgeous pottery and Paul Barlin does acrylics that are just stunning." I smiled up at him. "You are a genius. I knew there was a reason I married you."

"Thank you. But that still doesn't tell us where Evan is."

I glanced around. "No, it doesn't, does it? Where do you think he develops his prints? Or stores his equipment? It has to be somewhere here, you'd think."

"Good question."

We poked around and started opening what we'd assumed were closet doors until we found a small walk-in closet off the hallway. It must've been custom-built to take a corner of the garage and turn it into his darkroom.

It was a very tidy, organized space. There were shelves along the back wall where Evan's cameras were stored in a neat row, each one labeled carefully, all of the special lenses and attachments placed beside them.

"Hey, Matt."

"Yeah?"

"If Evan went on the run like the note in his truck implies, don't you think he'd take his cameras along, too? I mean he's clearly used to hiking with them given some of the photos he's taken. And if they're his livelihood I can't imagine him just abandoning them here. And I don't see space for more of them."

He nodded. "Good point."

"See? Someone really is trying to frame him."

"That's what it's starting to look like."

"You've gotta find him, Matt. Before whoever left that note does. I mean, assuming they didn't already and that the note wasn't just covering their tracks."

He pursed his lips. "Eh, I don't know that we've found enough for the Chief to change direction on this. But let me call my buddy Paul, see if he's willing to bring his tracking dog out. Do this off the books for now. He owes me one."

"Thank you."

I glanced around the place one more time. I really hoped nothing had happened to Evan. He was a man dealt a bad hand by life who'd somehow found a way to carry on and survive despite it. I hated to think that after all this time trying to find out the truth about Mary was going to ruin everything for him. That would be too bitter a pill to swallow.

CHAPTER 23

While Matt worked on getting his buddy Paul to help find Evan Browers, I went to talk to my grandpa.

He answered the door with a big hug and a smile. He was so excited about being a great-grandpa it was kind of funny. "Maggie May, come in. Lesley and I were just about to play a game of Scrabble. You want to join us?"

"Sure." It was not easy to beat my grandpa at Scrabble, but it was always fun to try.

We settled in around the dining room table and each drew our first tile. I got A so was able to play first. I almost played GNAW but I knew I'd regret wasting an N and G at the beginning of the game when I could save them to form a word with -ING at the end at some point later. Instead I played WAR.

My grandpa was not impressed. "You know we all have to play off of that, don't you?"

"Sorry, I had bad letters."

Lesley smiled at both of us and turned my WAR into BEWARE. "Better, Lou?"

"Better playing options, but a horrible use of your Es."

I suspected Lesley had made that play just to make him happy. "Grandpa, it's a game. Games are supposed to be fun."

He snorted. "Games are played to be won. Now. What brought you over? Pregnancy or murder investigation?"

"Murder investigation. Although, I was wondering, if it's not too much effort, could you build a crib for the babies? Or a rocker or something? I'd love to have something you made in their room."

My grandpa is an amazing carpenter. Some of the work he's done over the years is absolutely stunning. Multiple types of wood used to form beautiful patterns and designs. He's a master craftsman.

He gave me a shrewd look. "Are you sure that wouldn't violate your rule about jinxing the pregnancy?"

I'd told him and Lesley about not discussing baby names until our little bumps of joy were born and he'd laughed at me.

"I hope not. If I thought you could whip something together in a weekend, I'd probably wait to ask, but I know some of the things you do take a lot longer than that."

He smiled. "Just so happens I was working on some sketches of that very thing today. As long as you're sure you don't want some new-fangled creation that does ten things at once?"

"No. I'd much rather have something that reminds me of family."

"Consider it done. Now, what've you found out in that murder investigation of yours?"

I chewed on my lower lip, desperately wanting a Coke or ten but knowing I shouldn't. "Promise this stays in this room for now?"

He turned his full attention on me. "Why? What did you find out?"

I rubbed my chin. Where to start? "Mary Diever didn't go away to college. She went away to have a child."

"Was that nonsense still happening in the 80s?"

I shrugged. "It seems so. If you were a girl from a good family who didn't want your dad to know that you'd been knocked up, but also wanted to actually have the kid."

He took a sip of his coffee. "So she'd had a kid. How does that impact the murder investigation?"

"Well, she hid it from her father but he somehow found out right before her death."

He crossed his arms. "So you want to know if her father was the type to kill his daughter for shaming him?"

"No…Although, was he? Especially if she was thinking about reversing the adoption and raising the kid herself? Would he have tolerated something like that?"

He blew out a breath. "Her dad and her granddad were hard men. But I don't think either one would've killed her for something like that. Maybe very strongly encouraged her to change her plans. But not murder. I can't see it."

"That's what I kind of figured."

"So then why the visit?"

I gave him a sideways glance as I shuffled my tiles. "Because I think it's likely the baby's father killed her."

"And who was that?"

I laced my fingers together and pressed them to my mouth, still not sure telling him was a good idea. My grandpa sometimes has notions about the risks I should be taking.

"Maggie May. Who do you think was the father of the baby?"

I scrunched up my face. Best to just get it over with. "Looks like it was Quentin Baker."

He pushed back his chair and stood. "Drop this. Right now."

"Grandpa."

"I mean it Maggie May. Quentin Baker is a dangerous man."

"He's a senator."

"Exactly." He pressed his finger down on the table as he made his points. "Some men get that far because they have no major skeletons in their closet. But others get that far because they're ruthless at hiding or eliminating those skeletons. Which do you think he is given what you're investigating?"

When I didn't say anything, he shook his head. "You have to drop this. Quentin Baker is a man with money, power, and a lot to lose if this should come out."

I knew he was right, but I couldn't help arguing about it. "He's not even going to be in office anymore come next year. What does he really have to lose?"

"His reputation. All he has now is who he once was. If this comes out, he loses that." He stared me down. "Drop it."

"I'm not a dog grandpa. And Evan Browers will go to prison if I don't help him."

He reached for his non-existent cigarettes and then cussed under his breath when he was reminded once more that he no longer smoked.

I knew he wanted to tell me that Evan Browers didn't matter. But my grandpa also knew what prison was like, and he'd never wish that on anyone, especially an innocent man.

Well, at least not on anyone that didn't really deserve it.

"Let the police handle this, Maggie," he sank back in his chair.

"I can't."

"Why not?"

Reluctantly, I told him about the note they'd found in Evan's abandoned truck and the fact that he was missing.

"That is exactly why you need to drop this, Maggie May."

"But don't you see? No one else is going to believe Evan now. I'm his only hope."

My grandpa looked at me like I'd lost all my marbles. "Maggie May. Who exactly do you think arranged for Evan Browers to go missing and leave behind a confession?"

I hunched my shoulders. "Quentin Baker."

"My point exactly."

"But…"

"No buts, Maggie May." He shuffled his tiles so aggressively I expected one to fall off the rack. "You need to start thinking about your family. About those two little babies in your belly. Matt does, too. This isn't about you anymore. This isn't about your principles. This is about your family."

I pressed my lips together and shook my head. "But don't you understand? That's how the world goes to shit, Grandpa. People prioritize their own concerns at the expense of the greater good. Of the community. Of justice. And before you know it, we're living in a corrupt, cruel world where everyone justifies their most selfish instincts because everyone else is like that."

"You're damned right people prioritize themselves. Because most people are smart enough to realize that all championing the greater good does is gets them a whole lot of nothing. You try to do the right thing and you lose it all while the powerful still don't face any consequences. You can't win this fight, Maggie May. You have to focus on what matters." He glanced pointedly at my belly before he played his next word. "It's your turn. Play your tiles."

I fumed silently through the rest of the game. But surprisingly it either made me a better player or my grandpa a worse player, because for the first time in what felt like ages I beat him, by thirty points.

CHAPTER 24

Matt had a late shift that night, but I stayed up and waited for him to come home. (Well, actually, I took a bit of a nap on the couch while I waited to be honest. Pregnancy is hard.)

"Maggie, you waited up." He gave me a kiss on the cheek before removing all of his winter layers.

I nodded. "I needed to see your face."

He collapsed on the couch and rested his head on my lap, smiling up at me. "You know, pretty soon I'm not going to be able to do this. The bumps are going to take over and you're going to be as big as a house."

He looked so happy about it, I just had to laugh.

I sighed. "Twins. Someone up there has a sense of humor."

"Twin *girls*. We both got hit on this one. I wanted a girl, but two? We're in trouble." He smiled again. "They're going to wrap me around their little fingers. How do you feel about pony ownership?"

I laughed. "Fancy is as close as they're going to come to pony ownership. They may wrap you around their little fingers, but I will have final say on all dream vacations and purchases of live animals."

I ran my hand through his hair as we sat there in companionable silence. I was scared on so many levels, but so content, too.

Finally, I said, "Do you ever think about how if a murder isn't solved right away and you don't have anyone out there advocating for you then the person just gets away with it? I mean, I watch all these cold case shows and each time there's some mother or brother or father behind the case that called the police station every year on the day of the anniversary of the murder. Or hired a private investigator. Or did something else to not let the police forget. But if you don't have anyone to advocate for you, the person just…gets away with it."

He cupped my face in his hand. "We don't want to let the murderers go, but there's always a new one. Or if there isn't a new murder then there's other police priorities. We're starting to see an uptick in fentanyl deaths right now. Resources have to be used the most effective way they can."

I nodded. "I know why, but it's hard. To think of some poor girl like Mary Diever who no one fought for. Or Evan Browers. Have you found him yet?"

He shook his head. "No. Good news is there was no trail from the truck, which means it was a plant. Bad news is there was also no trail from his place. So wherever he went missing from, it wasn't home."

"I was hoping for better news."

"I know. So was I."

I nudged him off my lap. "Here, let's get you fed while we talk about what to do next."

He scarfed down leftover turkey casserole while I filled him in on my conversation with my grandpa. (I always go a little wild around Thanksgiving and buy myself a turkey even if I'm not hosting that year and then have to find some time to make the turkey before or after the actual day. This time I'd chosen before),

He didn't say anything until he was done eating and then he carefully set down his fork and sat back in his chair. "I hate to say it, but I agree with him, Maggie. Look what happened to Evan Browers. It would kill me if something happened to you, too."

Before I could object, he held up his hand. "I'm not going to let it go, I promise. I just want *you* safe."

I pressed my lips together. I trusted Matt. Not only with my life, but with my heart and my insecurities. And I didn't want to doubt him, but I wasn't sure he could pull it off. The Chief was a political man. And Matt had other more pressing priorities. I was the only one who was focused solely on this case.

At the same time, maybe I should play it a little safe. I mean, I was growing two little lives inside. But did backing off make me a coward?

Of course, was being a coward such a bad thing to be?

"Maggie," Matt squeezed my hand. "I'll take care of it, I promise."

After a long moment I said, "Okay." Part of being married is trusting your partner, so I decided I'd let it go.

For now.

(Because you don't tell a competent woman you'll take care of something if you aren't going to see it through. That's just an invitation for her to get angry and do it herself.)

I resolved to give Matt a chance to show me that he really would pursue the investigation. But if he didn't…Well, I wasn't going to sit around and watch some innocent man convicted for a crime he didn't commit if I could do anything about it.

CHAPTER 25

Over the next few days I tried not to think about the case. I really did. I threw myself into baby research instead. Being older and having twins, there was a lot to know on top of all the regular baby stuff.

Of course, all that made me do was pray daily that by the time I gave birth there'd be no risk in going down to Denver to deliver in a nice, big, sterile hospital that had a well-respected maternity ward and lots of medical supplies. That whole "let me float in a pool of warm water while soothing music plays in the background" approach to delivery was not for me, thank you very much.

Nope. Fill me up with drugs and use every trick in the modern medicine playbook to move things along, please.

So I really was trying to be good and forget about the case. Even when they finally found Evan Browers holed up in an abandoned cabin and arrested him for Mary's murder, I still kept my nose out of it. Barely.

But then the case came to me.

Because I bumped into Quentin Baker at the grocery store of all places. Granted, there's only one grocery store in the whole valley and with the entrances to the valley shut down there was no easy way to go elsewhere to shop, so it wasn't completely unexpected that we'd run into one another.

Then again, it had never happened in the year and a half I'd lived in Creek. And I certainly would've never expected him to turn in my direction when he saw me. It's not like we were on a wave-at-one-another-in-the-grocery-store basis.

"Maggie May Carver. Or is it Barnes now?" he asked as he walked up to me.

He was one of those politicians that embrace the good ol' boy look. He had on cowboy boots and jeans and a button-up denim shirt with one of those bolo ties that were probably never actually worn by any real cowboy.

The only part of the cliché he'd left off was the cowboy hat and the aw shucks attitude.

I casually moved so that the cart was between us. "It's Carver still. I kept my last name."

"Interesting choice, to continue to associate yourself with a known felon. I'd think you would've dropped your last name as soon as you could."

I met him eye-for-eye. I knew he was dangerous, but no one insults my family. "I chose that last name. And my grandpa may be an ex-felon, but he's the most stand-up man I've ever known. As a matter of fact, he has far more character and moral fortitude than most."

"Is that so?" His smile was positively smarmy.

"Yes. It is."

He studied me with cold gray eyes. "I heard you were looking into the Mary Diever murder."

"Who told you that?"

"I hear things."

"Then you probably know how far I got in that investigation, too. And know that I identified another suspect in her murder."

He stepped closer and I was glad for the cart between us. "I might have heard that. But of course, you've stopped that investigation now that the police have arrested Evan Browers, haven't you?"

I didn't answer him immediately, but finally I said, "Why did you do it? Why kill her? Was being powerful more important to you than that young girl's life?"

He forced a hearty laugh. "Is that what you think? That I'd dirty my hands that way? On a little bit of fluff?" He studied me for a long moment before placing his hands on the other side of the cart and leaning in. "You've lost a lot of people in your life, haven't you, Maggie? Your parents? Your fiancé?"

I didn't answer him. It took everything I had to stand there and not run. Never run from a predator. Rule one.

He gave me a big, hearty smile. "It's good that you've found someone now. Someone who makes you happy." He glanced down at my belly. "And that you're going to add to that. Children are priceless."

I crossed my arms against the shiver that ran up my spine. "Yes, they are. All children. Even Mary's."

He shook his head and laughed softly. "You know, I have a certificate on my wall that says the Bakers were one of the first families of Colorado. We have a long, proud history in this state. And I will do whatever it takes to ensure that history is not tarnished by some upstart nosy little busybody who came from nothing."

I held his gaze even though I really wanted to run. Or hit him. "You know what's funny? I've got one of those certificates, too, somewhere in a drawer. Because while your family was busy with their proud history of living off the backs of others, mine was down in Trinidad working the coal mines and cleaning the houses of rich folks like you. And if you think that puts you above us, you're wrong. My family has a proud history here, too. One where we don't bow down to the likes of you just because you tell us to."

He stepped back, still smiling his politician's smile. "We'll see about that. Be careful, Mrs. Carver. Hate to see you lose anyone else you love, but life can be tragic sometimes, can't it?" He winked as he turned away.

Only after he was out of sight did my brain catch up to my mouth. What had I just done? I knew better than to poke a bear.

CHAPTER 26

By the next day, I'd almost convinced myself that I'd overreacted to the conversation with Quentin Baker at the grocery store. I mean, really, he was a senator. Senators don't threaten people's families, do they? I'm sure I'd just imagined that. He was simply a man with a bad past who didn't want it brought up, that was all.

But then Matt didn't come home on time.

And when I called to ask where he was, the dispatcher couldn't reach him.

These things happen. A man needs to use the facilities, maybe he turns off his radio for a minute or two and forgets to turn it back on. Or he finds himself stuck in an area without reception.

But after twenty minutes, I started to panic. Fortunately, I was able to get Officer Clark on the line. I didn't like the man because he had it in for my grandpa (or at least he had), but he was a decent friend of Matt's. I knew he'd take it seriously.

I didn't tell him who had threatened my loved ones at the grocery store—I knew that would make him less likely to help me—but I did tell him that I'd been threatened the day before.

"Maggie, why do you always get involved in things you shouldn't?" he asked.

"Is this really the time for that conversation? Just find my husband, would you? Please. I need to know he's okay."

"Alright. I'll put out an alert for his vehicle, see if anyone can find it. Don't worry, it's probably nothing."

I paced the living room for the next thirty minutes as Fancy eyed me from her dog bed in the corner. She is not a fan of movement. She likes me to settle in one place so she can settle in a place nearby and snore. She probably would've fled to the backyard to get away from my pacing, but I'd blocked her in with me, just in case. A man who'd go after a pregnant woman's husband likely wasn't above going after a dog.

I almost jumped out of my skin when someone finally knocked on the door. It wasn't Matt, he would've just walked in. So who was it? I flung it open to see Officer Clark.

"What's happened? Where's Matt?"

He held his hands up like he was trying to calm a horse. "We don't know. We found his vehicle, abandoned. It was on the side of the road outside of Bakerstown."

"And? Why are you here? Why aren't you looking for him?" It took all of my self-control not to grab him and shake him.

"They're looking, don't worry." He licked his lips. "But I wanted to let you know as soon as possible. There was a bullet hole in the windshield."

Before I could faint, he grabbed my arm. "It was on the passenger side. No blood. We're pretty sure he wasn't hit."

Tears filled my eyes. "I can't lose him, Ben. I'm about to have twins and he needs to be here. He's gotta be the good parent. I'm…I can't…I can't do this. Not without Matt. You have to find him. I can't…"

I couldn't do any of it. Not just parenting, life. Getting through every day. I don't know how he'd done it but that good-looking, likeable, kind, intelligent, funny, you-know-what had made himself absolutely essential to me and I could not envision a life that didn't include him.

Ben stood there awkwardly, not quite knowing what to do in the face of a desperate, crying pregnant woman. You'd think they'd train cops to hug someone who's all distraught, but I'm pretty sure they actually train them to keep their distance and their hand on their weapon instead, which was the exact opposite of what I needed. It made me want to scream.

"Is there someone you want me to call?" he asked.

"My grandpa. Can you bring him over please? I don't want to leave in case they find Matt."

I could see that he didn't want to deal with my grandpa, but all he did was nod. "I'll go get him for you. Be right back. You'll be okay until then?"

"Yes. I'll be fine," I gritted out, directing all my fear into anger at men who treat women like breakable little dolls.

I swear, completely melt down in front of someone once and they never forget it.

"Okay. I'll be right back." He looked at me again like he wasn't sure I'd be okay for the amount of time it took him to go next door and come back, and I almost slammed the door in his face for it. But instead I nodded and smiled calmly back at him, trying to appear serene and calm so he'd get my frickin' grandpa already.

❧ ❧ ❧

It took another thirty minutes to locate Matt. Thirty of the most nerve-wracking, heart-wrenching moments of my life. I sat on the couch, chewing my thumbnail down to the quick (something I never do) while Lesley rubbed my back and told me it was going to be okay and my grandpa paced back and forth, clearly struggling not to tell me he'd told me so about Quentin Baker.

When they finally found Matt he was just fine. Seems when someone shot at my ex-military husband he took it personally and turned soldier. Which meant he'd parked his car, calculated an estimated trajectory for the bullet, and then went after the shooter, turning off his radio so the sound of anyone trying to reach him wouldn't give his position away.

The shooter had fled as soon as he realized what Matt was doing, but Matt grew up hunting and tracking in those woods, he wasn't about to be deterred. It just took him a little longer to catch the kid than he'd expected.

Yes, kid. Quentin Baker's sixteen-year-old great-nephew who insisted that he hadn't meant to shoot anyone. He'd just been playing in the woods and made a mistake. No intent to harm, especially not a cop.

Didn't even know who my husband was or I was. Just a weird coincidence that I was the one who wanted to accuse his great-uncle of murder and that said great-uncle had made veiled threats to my family the day before.

(Yeah, right.)

His very high-priced lawyer was all over things almost immediately. No way the kid was going to be charged with anything close to attempted murder which was very, very annoying.

But at the time I was a little more caught up in the realization that I was married to a cop, a man who risked his life at work every single day of his life. And not just because of me, either. Matt dealt with drunk drivers, drug users, abusers, fighters, killers. You name it. Each day there was a chance he wasn't going to come home to me.

As much as I wished it were the case, my husband wasn't out rescuing kittens out of trees and walking grandmas across the street.

Which is why I sobbed my little heart out on his shoulder when he finally got home to me. Seriously, you should never, ever mix life-threatening moments with pregnancy hormones.

Poor Matt. I'm pretty sure he did not know what on earth had happened to his competent, put-together wife. I mean, I'm normally solid when things go wrong. But it was just too much. All of it. Everything.

Fortunately, I was lucky enough to have married a man who was there for the tears just as much as he was there for the good parts. He sat with me on the couch and held me until I finally wound down. And then, bless the man, he offered to fix me whatever I wanted for dinner.

"You know what I really want?" I told him, still sniffling.

"What? Name it and it's yours."

"I'd really like a grilled peanut butter and jelly sandwich."

He chuckled. "I offer to fix you anything in the world and you ask for a grilled PBJ?"

"Please."

"Done." He kissed my forehead and went off to make

me the most perfect grilled PBJ in the world. I was so lucky to have him in my life.

CHAPTER 27

The next morning I woke up angry. You do not threaten my husband, I don't care who you are, and think you can get away with it. I'd thought about it most of the night as I lay in bed staring at the ceiling. There had to be a way to strike at Quentin Baker. And to do so in such a way that he never acted against my family again.

That meant exposing his secret.

As soon as it was a decent hour, I called Mason. I told him everything I'd found out about Mary Diever and Quentin Baker. And I told him how Quentin's great-nephew had shot at Matt. And how I wanted to make Quentin Baker pay for threatening my family.

"I don't care if he goes to jail for Mary Diever's murder, Mason. I want him ruined. How do we do that? How do we prove that he was the father of Mary's child? Publicly."

"Hmm. Good question."

I wanted to jump through the phone and throttle the man for sounding so coolly competent, but I needed him so I clenched my hand in my lap and waited while he thought it through.

Come on, man, figure it out, I silently fumed. *You're a sharp legal mind, you have to know how we can expose this. Get it together already.*

I didn't say any of that, though. I just calmly waited and practiced counting backwards from a thousand.

Finally, Mason spoke. "I think I have a possible solution. You said the woman Mary stayed with knows where to find the child?"

"Yes."

He thought about it another long, excruciating moment during which I refrained from screaming at him. "Hmm. Yes. I think it could work."

"What?" I finally snapped.

"Of course, the statute of limitations has passed. However, the case does not have to succeed to serve our purposes. We simply need a plausible reason to file."

"Mason. What case? What are you thinking?"

"Oh. I was thinking I can file suit on behalf of Mary's child to establish paternity. Usually the court only allows cases like that until the child is twenty-one. However, they have allowed cases in other states that were past the statute of limitations where there was a medical need to know. Which means I can probably make a general argument that the child needs to know paternity because he needs to know his medical risks. Although it would help if the child actually has a medical reason for pursuing the paternity case. At a minimum the filing will make public the fact that Quentin Baker may have been the father of Mary Diever's child."

I nodded. "Okay. Let's do this. And the initial filing will be public, right? If they somehow want to suppress the case, they have to counter-file to do so?"

"Yes. It will be a public record when it is filed. But I cannot guarantee it will stay public. Or that anyone will see the filing."

"But if we tip off the media about the filing they can find it before it's suppressed."

"Mm. Well. That can be a slippery slope. As an officer of the court…"

"Which I'm not. Look, no need for you to walk down that slope. As soon as you tell me you've filed, I'll find the filing and forward it to every investigative reporter I can think of. How will Senator Baker ever know that they didn't have a keyword search set for his name. He is a senator after all."

He hesitated for a moment and I thought he'd refuse to go through with it, but then he said, "What you do with knowledge of the filing is not my concern."

"Great. So what do you need to make this happen?"

"The name of the child. The child's agreement that I should make the filing. And a signed affidavit from the woman that Mary Diever stayed with about her encounter with Quentin Baker and her suspicion that he was the child's father. Get those for me and I'll make the filing."

"Done. I hope. How much do I owe you for this, Mason?"

Mason Maxwell was a very good lawyer, which meant he was not cheap. The only reason he wasn't already in possession of my entire life-savings was because he'd been sweet on Jamie when I needed his services last.

"Nothing. I never did like Quentin Baker."

"Excellent. I'll get the information today."

"I'll be ready to file as soon as you get it to me."

I hung up and smiled. Quentin Baker had messed with the wrong woman. And as soon as Mason made that filing everyone I loved would be safe again. Now I just had to convince Margie to tell me how to find Mary's son and had to convince the son to agree to file the suit. That should be…easy. (Or not.)

CHAPTER 28

At least I was calling Margie at a decent hour since Philly is on the east coast so a couple hours ahead of Colorado. After we exchanged the typical set of pleasantries and I filled her in on what had happened and why I was calling, I jumped right in.

"So you really thought you recognized Mary's kid? You know his name?" I asked.

"I did," she answered, wary, like she was regretting that she'd told me that and trying to figure out how to back away from it without lying to me.

"Could you give me the name, please?"

She was silent for so long I thought she might've walked away from the phone.

"Margie? We're trying to catch a killer here. Confirming that Quentin Baker was the father would help with that."

"I just, the scandal of it all. I'm not sure Mary's child deserves to go through that. He's happy. He has a good life. This could ruin all of that."

I sat up so fast, I startled Fancy who glared at me and took herself outside. "Wait. You know where he is *now*?"

"Well, of course. He did his residency at the hospital where I worked. We're connected on that Facebook thing. I doubt he sees any of my posts, he's a busy man. But I see his."

So Mary's son had become a doctor? Good for him.

"Do you happen to know if he's had any medical issues? Genetic ones? Or have his kids? Because that would be a legitimate reason he might want to track down his biological parents."

She sighed. "Yes, he has. He's actually been trying to find out who his parents were for about two years now."

"Really? Why?"

"Well, it seems during the genetic testing for his first child, he found out he was a carrier for Tay-Sachs disease."

I frowned. "That usually occurs in the Jewish population doesn't it?"

"Yes, ma'am. Which made him a little curious about his ancestry. Because the parents who raised him were definitely not Jewish. And it seems they had not told him he was adopted, bless their hearts. Of course, he obviously knows now after that whole Tay-Sachs scare. But he's had no success finding anything." I could almost hear her shrug through the phone. "Last I heard, he was going to try that DNA tracing through one of those national databases. Find his parents that way. Of course, from what you've told me, Mary and her whole family were dead before that became a possibility so I doubt he found anything useful. Maybe there was something that pointed towards his daddy, though…"

I stood up and paced the living room. "If there was, that would be perfect. Anything that points this direction adds to the case that Quentin Baker is the father. And the fact that he was already looking means he's more likely to be on board with our plan. It's perfect."

She was quiet on the other end of the line.

"What am I missing, Margie?"

"Well, it's just that…" she sighed. "I like the boy. But you have to understand that you contacting him like this is going to be a bit awkward for me."

"How so?"

"I told you, he's been looking for his parents for two years. And I knew all about Mary all that time. He may not take too kindly to finding out that I could have solved his issue long ago and I didn't say anything."

"Mm. Fair point. How about you give me his name and phone number and I keep you out of it?"

"But you said you're gonna need that affidavit from me about what I saw between Mary and Senator Baker."

"True. But maybe we can list you as a Jane Doe due to your ongoing involvement in helping battered women flee their partners. It's worth a shot. And it'll at least give you time to figure out how to square things with him."

"That might work. I still feel bad for the boy. Looking for his mama only to find out she was murdered and his daddy might have been the one to do it."

I nodded. "It's definitely not the end he would've hoped for, I'm sure. But then again, this is someone he never actually knew. He has no emotional connection to her like you or I might to the mothers who raised us."

"True…" She sighed again.

"Margie. I need him to file this case so I can protect my family. Can I please have the name?"

"Fine. Might as well. It's in God's hands now."

CHAPTER 29

I was lucky. It was Dr. Brian McKendrick's day off. (That was the name of Mary's son.) So when I called his cellphone he actually answered. Which was another small miracle, because there is no way I am answering my phone if I don't recognize the number. But as a heart surgeon it seemed Dr. McKendrick was a little more open to calls from strangers.

There was no easy way to start the conversation I needed to have, so I just went right for it.

"Dr. McKendrick, my name is Maggie Carver, I live in Colorado, and I believe I know who your parents were. I'd like your help in proving that."

"How did you get my name? Or my number? This is a private number."

"I was given them by someone who knew your mother. And recognized you as her son. Can I have a minute to explain. Please?"

He hesitated for a moment, which I can't blame him for. Someone calls you up out of the clear blue and claims to know who your mother was, it has to set off about a million alarm bells. Either that or you're the type of person who falls for every "free trip" scam there is.

"Dr. McKendrick. Please. It's important that I get your help on something related to all of this. Don't worry, I don't want money. It's…Just let me explain?"

I could hear his wife in the background asking what was going on, but he must've waved her off because soon it grew quiet. "Okay. You have five minutes. Go."

I took a deep breath. Where to start?

"Alright. As I told you, my name is Maggie May Carver. I live in Creek, Colorado. Recently a man asked me to look into a thirty-six-year-old murder where he was the accused. The woman who was murdered is the woman I believe was your mother. As part of the investigation I found out that she went away to Philadelphia to give birth to you and then gave you up for adoption."

I paused, waiting for the inevitable questions.

"So you're an investigator?"

"Not exactly. I just happen to have gotten involved in a few investigations here or there and it made the paper so now other people ask for my help, too, sometimes."

I doodled on my notepad, giving him time to absorb all of this and ask more questions.

"Who was my mother then? And how can you be so certain?"

"You have a port-wine stain on your neck, right? And fairly distinctive gray eyes?"

"Yes."

"Well, the woman that Mary stayed with when she was pregnant was a nurse. And she saw you at your birth and then she saw you at the hospital after you'd been adopted. And later she worked with you when you became a doctor."

"Who?"

"I'm not at liberty to say. She's helping me out by putting me in touch with you and I need to respect that. Hopefully she'll tell you herself at some point since Mary did live with her for about nine months."

"You keep saying Mary. Is that my mother?"

"Yes, Mary Diever."

"What was she like?"

"Everyone said she was very nice. Very pretty. Quiet. Kept to herself. A good person." (I decided he didn't need to know the rest of it.)

"Do you have any photos?"

"Only one or two. Unfortunately, shortly after she died, her father and grandfather also died and her mother had passed away years before so there really wasn't family left to keep things like that."

"And you said she was murdered?" he asked, tentatively.

"Yes. About six months after you were born."

"Why call me? You said you needed my help. This isn't just you being a nice person." It was clear he still didn't trust me, which was fine. I wouldn't have trusted me either.

I bit my lip. Moment of truth time. "True. I called you because I suspect that your biological father is the one who murdered Mary because she changed her mind about giving you up for adoption."

"What would he care?"

"He was married at the time." I cleared my throat. "And had kids and political ambitions. He was about twenty years older than her. I don't think those ambitions could've survived the scandal."

"So he killed her?"

"Maybe. Yes. If nothing else, it's another suspect for the cops to look at other than the man who loved your mother and would've helped raise you if she'd been able to get you back."

He was silent for a long moment. "This is a lot to take in. And I still don't understand what you want from me."

"Well…" I took a deep breath. How to explain this in a way that would get him on board? "I would like you to file a paternity suit to prove that the man is your father."

"Why? Can't I just reach out to him and ask if he's my father? Why do I have to file a lawsuit?"

"Because the fact that he is the father would still be a scandal. And I think he would want to hide that and is willing to hurt people to do so."

He scoffed at that. "Look, lady, I don't know you. And I don't believe you."

"Someone shot at my husband the other day. After this man threatened me and told me to drop my investigation."

"And you want me to prove this man is my father?" He laughed once. "Why? He doesn't know who I am, I'm safe. Filing this lawsuit will risk my family. And for what?"

"To help get justice for your mother. A young lady who was scared as could be, but still chose to give birth to you even though she knew it would upset the father of her child."

He didn't respond.

"Please. The only way I can protect my family is by making this public. Until it's public, I'm a danger to this man and he will try to stop me. Once it's public, there's nothing to hide anymore."

"I'm not a lawyer, but I'm pretty sure something like this will get squashed pretty fast."

"Not fast enough. Your dad is a public figure. We're going to…*I'm* going to, make sure that the news knows as soon as the filing hits. It will be out there before they can suppress it."

"Who is my dad?" he asked, suddenly wary.

I grimaced, but he'd have to know sooner or later. "Senator Quentin Baker."

"That man is my dad? He's vile."

"Well…yeah."

He was silent for a long moment. "I need to think about this."

"Please don't think too long. We're in danger until you make that filing. And I…I just found out I'm pregnant? With twins? I really don't want anything to happen to us or to the babies' father. Or to my dog. Or my grandpa. I mean, I'm not giving this up. I'll find a way with or without you to bring your mother justice, but I'd really like the people I love to be safe while I do so."

Another long stretch of silence. "What would I have to do? How much will it cost?"

"It's free because I have a lawyer-friend who really doesn't like the man. All you have to do is agree to be part of the suit. And provide your DNA if it comes to that."

When he didn't immediately respond, I added, "My nurse friend said you'd tried posting your DNA to some of those sites? Did anything point to Colorado?"

"Yeah. But it was fourth or fifth cousins. Nothing too close."

"Well, the family has been here for over a hundred years. The other side, your mother's side, was actually

Philadelphia."

"There were results for Philly, too. But again, only fourth or fifth cousins."

"I think your mom was an only child of an only child, so makes sense."

I didn't want to end the call, not without him agreeing to help. But I'd stretched things as far as I could. "Do you mind if I get those DNA results from you? And I can send you the pictures I do have of your mom if you want."

"I had a private lab do the sequence so I can send that to you. Police should be able to use it. And, yeah, I'd appreciate the photos."

"And you'll think about the case?" I didn't want to beg, but I would've if I thought it would help.

"How certain are you that he's my father? This isn't some stupid political stunt is it?"

"No. Not at all. That nurse friend who gave me your name saw them together shortly before you were born. She was pretty convinced he was the father. And you guys have the same eyes, according to her. But that's all I have, which is why the DNA is so important."

"So we could be ruining some man's life for nothing?"

"He did also threaten me at the supermarket and his great-nephew did put a bullet through the windshield of my husband's car. I mean, it's circumstantial, but there are some clear signs there I think."

He was quiet for another long, long moment.

Finally, he said, "Okay. Fine. Let's do it. We'll find out one way or another. And if he isn't my father, maybe this will make someone come forward with new information on the man who really is."

"Thank you. Thank you so much." If we'd been in person, I would've hugged him.

"I just hope you're right."

"Me, too."

I jotted down his email and got off the phone as fast as I could before he changed his mind.

CHAPTER 30

My next call was to Mason Maxwell, but that's where we hit a bit of a snag.

"Mason Maxwell," he answered, clearly distracted and not wanting to be on the phone.

"Mason, everything okay?"

"Maggie. Right. I was supposed to call you. You need to get to Greta's."

"Greta's? Why?" I stood up, looking around for I wasn't even sure what.

"Jamie went into labor."

"Already? But it's too early. Are you sure it was labor and not just those fake contractions pregnant women get sometimes?"

That seemed to settle him because the note of panic left his voice. "Positive. She gushed all over the foyer when her water broke."

"Well where is she now? Why aren't you with her?" I barely refrained from adding, *What kind of husband are you to be telling me to get over there when you're not there yourself?*

He calmed even further. Seems my being obnoxious

is sometimes a good thing. "She's at Greta's. I took her over there but then we realized we'd forgotten everything. Our go bag, my computer, her phone, her purse. Everything. We ran to the car without even thinking. So I had to come back here."

"Mason, you don't need your computer when your wife is in labor."

"You do when you're an attorney who has a hearing at ten."

I let my silence speak for me.

"Jamie is the one who told me to come back home and get it. She said she's fine."

"This is Jamie we're talking about. She'll probably say she's fine right up until the baby pops out. I bet you money if her water hadn't burst she would've waited until the last possible moment to go over to Greta's."

"You're probably right. Which is why you need to get over there right now. Because that hearing is in ten minutes and there's no way I'm going to make it back to her before it begins."

"Mason!" I had really been hoping there'd be a snowstorm or something when Jamie went into labor that would let me politely decline having to be there for the big event. And now I might be there but Mason wouldn't? "What is wrong with you?"

"I do not want to miss the birth of my first child. But I have to attend this hearing. I will try to get it postponed and will hopefully be there within the hour, but right now if you can get there, please do."

I really wanted to make up excuses for why I couldn't go, but I also didn't want Jamie to have to give birth without her husband or her best friend there. "Fine. I will get in my van and head right over to Greta's. By the way, I have a name for you for the lawsuit against Quentin Baker."

"Good. If we have time between when I arrive and the actual delivery I can get that filed while we're waiting."

I wanted to tell him to wait, that Jamie was more important, but at the same time...Labor can take *hours* and it was my family's safety on the line. The sooner Mason managed to make the filing, the better.

"Okay. See you at Greta's."

I hung up, grabbed a change of clothes, food for Fancy, food for me, and Fancy and I were out the door in five minutes flat.

My best friend was having a baby. Holy...

CHAPTER 31

I desperately wanted a Coke to accompany me on my drive to Greta's, but I was a good girl and took a water bottle filled with mint tea instead. (It had that same bite to it that I liked in Coke so it made my lack of my favorite beverage more manageable.)

Fancy stood at my shoulder the whole drive, staring out at a sky that threatened snow. It wasn't clouded or anything, but there's a certain cold haze that develops sometimes right before a snowstorm. So we had blue sky but misted, like seeing it through a frosted glass pane.

I pulled up in front of Greta's mansion (it's very Italian-feeling with its circular driveway and central fountain and two wings leading off of the main entranceway) and took a moment to breathe. I could do this. I needed to be strong for Jamie. She couldn't see me freaking out or else she might freak out, too.

This was normal. Women had babies all the time. It was no big deal. Haha. Right. The lies we tell ourselves.

I might've stayed in the van for another hour or ten, but Fancy started crying her head off, demanding to be let out.

Jamie met us at the door with a big smile. She grabbed my hands. "I can't believe it's time already."

"Neither can I. Are you sure? I mean, don't they sometimes try to just put you on bed rest or whatever if your water breaks early? I thought that's what I read the other day."

(I'd been doing far too much reading up on early deliveries since finding out about my own little bumps of joy.)

"They can, yes. Especially if the baby won't do well being born too early. But Dr. Dillon thinks I'm close enough to term not to worry about it. She said it might be a different story if they had to induce contractions, but no need there." She sort of grimaced. "This little guy is determined to come out today."

She stepped outside. "The doctor wants me to walk around for now. Will you walk with me?"

"Outside? Shouldn't you stay close to the delivery room? Because I am not prepared to help you give birth in the woods."

She laughed and then winced, bending over in pain. "Ooof. Those things are painful."

"Was that a contraction?"

She nodded and slowly stood back up. "They're still pretty far apart. We have time. Come on."

"If you say so…"

As we walked down the path that led around the side of Greta's mansion, I added, "You know, I kind of think Evan and Abe have the better end of this one. Hire a surrogate, let her sacrifice her entire body for ten months and go through the pain and risk of delivery, and then voila, baby in hand. Easy peasy. I really think that's the optimal way to do this thing."

Jamie laughed and shook her head. "Oh no. You just wait until you feel that first little kick. Then you'll understand how the pregnancy portion is just as magical as the parenting portion."

"If you say so." Me, I personally preferred the idea of parenthood without life-threatening risk and intense pain. Ah, to be a man.

I glanced up at the leaden sky, wondering what we'd do if Jamie went into labor before anyone could arrive to help. Because once that storm closed in, we were probably on our own.

"By the way," I said, "Doctor Dillon is here already, right? This isn't a 'call me when we get closer' situation is it?"

"Yes, Doctor Dillon is already here. Along with my doula, Ruth. And a nurse. Unfortunately, there's no birthing pool. Greta didn't get it in time. And, given the fact my water burst early, no one is comfortable with my taking a non-standard approach. So I'm stuck with the whole feet-in-stirrups thing."

"What about an epidural?"

"Nope. Don't want one."

"Jamie…"

"I don't want one."

She stared me down until I changed the subject. As we wandered our way around Greta's backyard for the next half hour we talked about the pet resort and my idea to use Evan Browers' photography. Jamie suggested we could maybe do Colorado wildlife-themed menu items both in the barkery and the café although we'd need to make sure it didn't tip over into too kitschy given our target clientele. We wanted upscale hunting lodge not theme park.

(You can charge twice as much that way for the same thing.)

She also knew a ton more local artists who could be part of the art gallery. The more we talked about that idea the more excited I was for it. That would definitely be upscale if we set it up right.

As we turned for another loop of the backyard, a police car with flashing lights and Mason's black Lincoln pulled into the driveway. Matt and Mason hopped out of their respective vehicles, both grinning.

Mason made a beeline for Jamie. "Are you okay? How far apart are the contractions? Have you been doing your breathing? How long until the baby is here?"

Jamie laughed. "Maybe you should practice your own breathing, babe. I'm fine. We have time. Go file that case so Maggie and Matt will be safe."

He hesitated.

"Go." She shoved him away, laughing.

"Don't worry," I said. "I'll bring her inside so you won't be haunted by worries about her giving birth in the woods." Like I was.

He stared at me. "That would be horrible."

"I know. That's why I'm going to bring her inside. Right now."

Jamie laughed. "I'm fine you two. I am not going to give birth out here, I promise. Now, go."

As Mason turned back towards the house, Jamie sucked in a breath through her teeth.

"Another contraction?" I asked as we both smiled at Mason as he glanced back at us.

"Yep."

"How many have you had while we were walking around out here?"

"A few."

"So we really should get you inside, then?"

"Mmhm. Yeah, that would be good."

Matt who'd been on his phone, joined us just then. "Can I help?"

"Yes. We need to get Jamie inside. You walk on one side, I'll walk on the other. Just in case."

As he took his position on Jamie's other side, he grinned at me. "This is going to be us soon, you know."

"Do not remind me."

I glanced at Greta's house. I was sure she had state-of-the-art facilities, but giving birth in a room of my friend's house was not something I wanted to experience. Ever. Ah well, at least it wasn't the good old days when women gave birth in their marriage bed. Ugh. That didn't even bear thinking about.

CHAPTER 32

We escorted Jamie upstairs and down the hall to the delivery room. It was very nice. There was everything you'd expect to see, including what I presumed was a baby warmer in the corner. Dr. Dillon was there and smiled at us as we came into the room.

"Contractions getting closer together?" she asked.

Jamie nodded through one. "Yes. I'm thinking it might be time."

"Well, climb on up on the table and let's see."

"I'll just go get Mason," I said, trying to make my escape.

"No." Jamie grabbed my arm with so much force I was pretty sure I was going to lose it if I tried to pull free. "Don't leave me alone. Matt can get him."

I turned to Matt, silently pleading for him to rescue me, but he nodded instead. "Will do. I'll be right back."

"Matt…" But he was gone. Nothing to do but tuck myself away at the head of the bed where I wouldn't have to see any of…whatever was going on down below. There's being friends and then there's things you just don't need to see.

I appreciated that Jamie thought I should be there in that moment. And that I *could* be there for her in that moment. But delivery is not something you really want to be present for, you know?

I mean, even cheery, happy types like Jamie crack under the pressure. And to know that I was going to have to go through that in a few months? Yeah, not something I wanted to witness.

But Jamie wasn't letting go. And by then my trying to run for the door meant running past whatever Dr. Dillon was up to in the baby area. So I sucked it up and tried to keep a never-ending nonsensical conversation going with Jamie instead.

I was about to bolt and drag Mason into the room by his ear when he finally arrived. "It's time?" he asked.

Uptight, buttoned-up, never-a-hair-out-of-place, Mason Maxwell, looked nervous.

Dr. Dillon smiled at him. "It's time."

Now, let me tell you that when they say, "it's time" they don't always mean what you think they do. Because, me, I think, okay, we'll be done with this in about five minutes or so, right? Just push a few times and there's the baby.

Oh no. That is not how it goes. That just means the straining, pushing, gasping cacophony has begun.

Don't ask me how long it actually took. But it was no five minutes. Or if it was five minutes it was some purgatory-style version that never ended.

Lucky Matt got to hang out somewhere with Greta. Me, I got to have my hand nearly torn off by Jamie. Mason did, too, except he was grinning like a happy fool the whole time.

At the end Jamie was a red-faced, sweating mess and I'd learned a few new, highly creative and definitely not realistic phrases to use when I was mad at someone.

I would tell you the baby was beautiful when it was born—and ultimately he was, Jamie and Mason make very good-looking kids—but fresh out of the womb? No. Not so much.

That whole expelling a child from your body thing is very messy. And that boy was a squaller. Had some lungs on him. And a face as reddened as his mama's was at that point.

Not that Jamie or Mason noticed, not one bit. The adoration on their faces…It was like someone had slipped them both the best drug in the world and they were flying high as high could get.

I freed my broken hand and stepped outside to let them have their moment. I was so happy for them. But, wow, what a process.

I found Matt snoozing in a chair about ten feet down the hall. I kicked his foot. "Wake up. It's over."

"Yeah?"

I nodded.

"What do you think?"

"I think someone better invent a magic technology that transports these two out of my belly without any of that or I'm not going to make it."

He pulled me onto his lap and kissed me. "You'll be fine."

"Says the man who does not have to do this."

"No. Worse. I have to stand there helpless while you perform a miracle."

I side-eyed him. "I should call you on that worse part,

but the rest of it was pretty good." I rested my head against his shoulder. "You want to see the baby?"

"In a minute." He cuddled me closer and I closed my eyes, so glad to have him in my life.

🐾 🐾 🐾

When we finally walked back into the room, the baby had been cleaned and bundled up. Mason was holding him, a dopey smile on his face.

"You want to hold him?" he asked, looking at me.

I held my hands up to keep him back. "Oh no. I wouldn't want to break him. Me and babies, you know."

He laughed. "You sure you don't want to practice now before you're trying to juggle newborns?"

I just stared at him. He was right. *I* was going to have to juggle *two* of them. Two, tiny, small, fragile, breakable little babies. How was I going to do that?

"Any chance you'd like to raise three kids instead of one?" I asked, only half-kidding. "We'll take the twins back when they're about, say, nine months old. That's a fun period with kids, I think. Right?"

Matt laughed. "I'll hold him."

And he did. Frickin' natural. Didn't even need to be told what to do, he automatically had one big hand cradling the head and the other cradling the body. That little baby snuggled up against his chest like it was home.

"See? Not too hard," he said.

"Yeah. Not too hard at all," I mumbled semi-hysterically. "I'm just gonna…Go down the hall…Find Greta…Tell her about the baby…Yeah. That. I'll, I'll be back."

I fled.

CHAPTER 33

We all ended up crashing at Greta's that night because the snowstorm moved in and it was a doozy.

Fancy had managed to find the baby, who Jamie and Mason had named Mason Maxwell, Jr. (Max for short). She posted herself right in front of wherever Max was and kept a careful eye on anyone who approached. It was a bit awkward, but definitely cute.

I finally had to lock her in our room when it came time to go to bed or I think she would've stayed there the whole night.

The next morning the paternity filing against Quentin Baker was all over the news. Mason had managed to get his filing in before Jamie went into labor and Matt had conveniently sent a copy of it to every major news outlet in the state while he was waiting in the hallway.

By the time we all gathered in Greta's kitchen for a breakfast casserole, fresh orange juice, and coffee it had hit the national news. Mason's phone was blowing up. He ignored most of the calls, but then he flashed us all a smile and answered.

"Mason Maxwell."

I could hear the sound of someone screaming on the other end of the line.

"Quentin, there is a very easy way to prove you are not the father. Simply submit your DNA. Then you can call the press and tell them we had it wrong, that this was just a political witch hunt meant to smear your name."

There was more shouting from the other end of the line.

"You can try that, but I should tell you that It is only defamation if it is not true."

He set the phone back down, smiling. "He hung up. Don't know why. Must have been something I said."

Matt offered to take Max while Jamie and Mason were eating. They already looked exhausted and it was only the first day. But they were both so clearly happy, leaning into one another with soft little smiles on their faces, too, that I couldn't help but smile at them.

I nudged Matt with my hip. "Well, at least one of us will be able to hold our children without breaking them in the first few months," I quipped. "All we have to do is teach you how to nurse and we are set."

He smiled at me, his expression all soft and warm. "I can do the night feedings. Although, juggling two might be a bit of a trick. But you give me a bottle, I'm happy to help."

"And you'll do diapers, too?" I asked, skeptical.

"Of course. They're our children, aren't they? It's as much my responsibility to raise them as it is yours."

I kissed him on the cheek, careful not to disturb the baby. "I picked well when I picked you."

He chuckled softly. "I'm the one that did the picking, not you. You were just smart enough to succumb to my charms."

I laughed. "Well. Not sure smarts had anything to do with it. You overwhelmed me with your…regard."

I rested my head on his shoulder, watching the baby sleeping peacefully, his little face scrunched up. "So, what happens now? With the Mary Diever case?"

I knew he'd talked to his Chief earlier.

"Good news is the paternity suit cast enough doubt on Evan Browers being the killer that the Chief has agreed to release him and hold off on anything further with respect to him for now. We're filing today to compel Quentin Baker to give us a DNA sample. The paternity suit gave us enough probable cause to ask for it."

"I'm surprised the Chief backed off so easily."

He smiled and moved the baby around to make him more comfortable. "It probably helped that I told him Mason Maxwell was going to be the attorney representing Browers if he went forward."

"Is he?" I glanced across the table at Mason who was looking at us in surprise.

"Probably not. But it worked." Matt's phone started to ring.

"Here. Take the baby." Before I could stop him, Matt turned and nestled the baby against my chest, placing my hands for me. "Officer Barnes," he said, answering the phone as he abandoned me.

The baby started to fidget and I froze. What was I supposed to do? What if I tried to adjust my grip and dropped him? Mason and Jamie would never forgive me. And somehow I didn't think offering them one of my twins would fix it.

(I'm kidding. Obviously only a psychopath would even think about trying to give away one of their children, and I'm clearly not that, right? Ahem. Right.)

"Jamie," I called out softly, trying not to move. "You should probably take him back now."

She laughed. "Okay. Give him over." She held out her hands.

"Uh…Can you…I'm not sure what to…"

Greta reached over and plucked him out of my arms. "You are so funny, Maggie. Have you never held a baby?"

"No, not really. I never had siblings. And I've managed to avoid holding my friends' kids until they were older."

"This must be fixed. You must be ready when the twins come, no?"

I sighed. "Yeah. That's probably a good idea. Maybe I can get one of those fake babies from the high school. Do they still do that sort of thing?"

Jamie shook her head. "You don't need a fake baby, Maggie, you can hold Max."

Before I could say "do I have to", Matt hung up the phone and I desperately transferred my attention to him. "Any news?"

"We've been getting some interesting phone calls this morning since the paternity story broke. Seems there might have been a couple of witnesses who didn't realize what they saw at the time. Chief wants me to go interview them." He kissed me on the forehead. "And, sorry, but this is now police-only. Too high-profile to have you involved."

I wanted to object, but it made sense. "Okay. See you at home tonight?"

"See you then."

CHAPTER 34

Once the dominos started to fall, they really started to fall. But not exactly in the direction I thought they would.

The court compelled Quentin Baker to submit a DNA sample that same day. His lawyers fought it, but they only bought an extra two days for him and then the crime lab put a rush on the results because it was such a national story.

By the end of the week the results were back. Quentin Baker was in fact Brian McKendrick's father. The source of the Tay-Sachs, though, had to be Mary Diever because there wasn't a trace of it in the DNA for Baker.

Further digging by McKendrick unearthed the fact that his grandmother had very likely been from a Jewish family in Philadelphia but had run away when she turned eighteen. She'd been the only child of an only child so it wasn't definitive, but it made the most sense family tree-wise.

And those calls that started pouring in shed a whole new light on Senator Baker. Seems he'd made a pattern of targeting the quiet daughters of men he knew. Mary

Diever was not the first nor was she the last. By the end of it all, sixteen women had come forward.

All said he had a temper. All felt they couldn't tell their families about it because he had one form of leverage or another over their families that he threatened to use.

There were no other illegitimate children, though. Brian was the only one.

Where things got interesting was when it came to figuring out who the killer was. Likely even with the testimony of those sixteen women, Mary Diever's murder would've remained unsolved. It's a big jump to make from aggressive ex-lover to murderer especially without physical evidence or witnesses.

But it turned out the murder weapon was in Senator Baker's office. At that point it looked like a slam dunk case. Use Brian's DNA to match to Mary's blood on the rock, tie it via circumstance to the senator, and all done. Except…

Senator Baker hadn't been in town when Mary Diever was killed. But his wife had. His wife who then gifted him a big, ugly rock as a book end and informed him he needed to do a better job of cleaning up his own messes next time around.

He, of course, threw her under the bus the minute the police found the rock. (Why he hadn't disposed of it when I started snooping around, I do not know, but maybe thirty-six years without being caught had made him sloppy. Or forgetful of what that rock might reveal.)

But he didn't get off. He'd known who killed her after all. It was all very headline-worthy and scandalous, but I was just glad that my family was safe, including my not-quite-as-little-as-they-had-been bumps of joy.

EPILOGUE

Thanksgiving Day is my favorite holiday. I know it has a fraught history in this country and that's why some don't like it, but for me personally it was never really about any of that. I identify with the Pilgrims about as much as I identify with that patch of something behind the fridge that really needs to be cleaned up if I ever get around to it, which means not at all.

For me Thanksgiving is about two things: spending time with the people I love and good food.

Let me tell you about the food we had first.

There was a turkey with its crispy, golden skin and juicy flesh stuffed with stuffing made using my super-secret recipe that had come down through my mom's side of the family. It involved giblets. Which meant hours of preparation just so those little suckers could be diced up and thrown in with the usual bread and celery and onions and what-not to give it that extra-rich flavor.

I know they don't think you should stuff a turkey these days, but I'm about as on board with that notion as I am with the idea that you can't taste-test chocolate chip cookie batter as you're preparing it.

Yeah, yeah, salmonella, food poisoning, blah, blah, blah. I didn't care. I wanted my stuffed turkey. And of course I snuck off the crunchy bit at the end when it was all done just for myself. (Which I shared with Matt, that's how strong our love is. Some people may be willing to die for their spouse. *I* am willing to share the crunchy bits of the turkey stuffing.)

We also had green bean casserole. Not the fancy kind that people try to create and ruin the whole thing. No, we had the real deal. The good old-fashioned, cooking with canned products version. Dump in two cans of green beans, follow that with some mushroom soup, make sure you have plenty of crispy fried onions mixed in there, and…Perfection.

And there were mashed potatoes. So simple to create, but oh so good.

And gravy. Lots and lots and lots of gravy to smother it all with.

And cranberry sauce. Again, nothing fancy. No homemade mess. Just that smooshed-up, canned version that plops onto a plate.

(Truth be told, I could easily eat an entire can of cranberry sauce all by myself which is why I had four extra cans of it at home.)

That right there was the core of my Thanksgiving meal. Trish had made sweet potato pie and Lesley had made a macaroni bake and there was bread, of course. And deviled eggs. And stuffed celery. And pie. So much pie. Pumpkin and pecan and lemon chiffon.

(Don't ask about the lemon chiffon. Not a traditional choice, but some sort of joke between Matt and Jack that dated back to their childhood. They'd both brought one, so it must be a good joke, but neither would say more about it.)

Of course, it wasn't about the food (even though I love the food). I've had other Thanksgivings where we had ham instead. Or pork roast. And once I even went out with a friend for a fancy French meal where we ate duck. Those were all good Thanksgivings, too.

Because they had the part that really matters. The people.

Some years it's family, some years it's friends, some years it's both. But it's companionship and laughter and joy that we're all here for another year. All able to be together. (Sometimes just in spirit and that's okay, too.)

My grandpa and Lesley were there. And Jack and Trish and Sam. And Matt. And Fancy.

And Evan Browers. Because that man deserved a new start. My grandpa pressed his lips together when I told him I'd invited Evan, but he also took him aside after the meal and they had a good long talk. My grandpa knows all about giving people second chances.

I knew he'd opened up to Evan when he invited him to a friendly game of Scrabble.

Thanksgiving is about seeing what you have and appreciating it for what it is. It's not a day for regrets or wanting something more.

It's about being in that particular moment with those particular people and being grateful to be there.

Life never works out the way we want. That year was certainly testament to that fact, for us and for the world.

But I couldn't see the point in looking at what we hadn't had—like the long, luxurious honeymoon to some exotic locale that I'd dreamed of—when I had something far more important in my life. Love. Acceptance. Community.

And a chance to make it even better the next year.

I looked around that table at all those smiling faces and I was content, if just for a moment.

ABOUT THE AUTHOR

When Aleksa Baxter decided to write what she loves it was a no-brainer to write a cozy mystery set in the mountains of Colorado where she grew up and starring a Newfie, Miss Fancypants, that is very much like her own Newfie, in both the good ways and the bad.

You can reach her at aleksabaxterwriter@gmail.com or on her website aleksabaxter.com.

Printed in Great Britain
by Amazon

74658829R00108